Remembering his kindness to her grandfather, Lyall suddenly felt ashamed of the way she'd treated him. Taking a step towards him, she said, 'Before you go, I would like to thank you for . . .'

'There's no need for thanks,' he broke in.

'But there is.' Lyall lifted grave green eyes to his face. 'You were marvellous to Grandad.' Seeing a slight twist to his lips, she added in a small voice, 'And to me. I don't understand why you went to so much trouble.'

'I wanted to.'

'But why?'

'Because I intend to marry you.' Jordan spoke so casually that she doubted her own hearing.

She stared at him in confusion. He didn't look as if he was joking. 'We've only just met,' she protested. 'You scarcely know me.'

MOTIVE FOR MARRIAGE

BY

LEE WILKINSON

MILLS & BOON LIMITED
ETON HOUSE 18–24 PARADISE ROAD
RICHMOND SURREY TW9 1SR

All the characters in this book have no existence outside the imagination of the Author, and have no relation whatsoever to anyone bearing the same name or names. They are not even distantly inspired by any individual known or unknown to the Author, and all the incidents are pure invention.

First published in Great Britain 1987
by Mills & Boon Limited

This edition 1988

ISBN 0 263 75903 2

Set in Baskerville 10 on 11¾ pt.
05-0488-48500

Computer typeset by SB Datagraphics,
Colchester, Essex

Printed and bound in Great Britain by
Collins, Glasgow

CHAPTER ONE

'THERE's no earthly use sitting and brooding,' Mitch said crisply. 'It's over a month now since Paul died. Time you snapped out of it and started to fight back. Jameson's party will be a good start. Come on, make up your mind to go.'

Mitch, who worked in the accounts department at Jameson's Electronics, was small and curvaceous with bright gold fluffy hair and forget-me-not blue eyes. Beneath the shallow, dumb-blonde image she projected, she was shrewd and good-hearted, loyal and compassionate, and very, very determined.

But never in all her life had Lyall felt lower. Paul's death, on top of everything else, had shattered her. He'd been so young, only three years older than herself, so handsome, capable of such gaiety and charm. It didn't seem possible that all that life and vitality could have been wiped out so swiftly, so *horribly*.

Shocked and disbelieving, she had read of the crash in the morning paper. An eye witness had reported that the driver had still been alive and conscious, after smashing his car into the concrete pier of a road bridge, but, possibly dazed by the impact, had seemed unable to release his seatbelt before the petrol tank had exploded. Horrified onlookers who had rushed to help had been driven back by the flames and intense heat.

'Well?' Mitch persisted, fixing the younger girl with a beady eye.

Lyall shook her head and said with quiet desperation, 'I can't . . . I just can't.'

'It isn't as if you loved him.'

'If only I *had*, the accident might never have happened.'

'For God's sake, don't start blaming yourself!' Mitch cried fiercely. 'You couldn't love him just because he wanted you to. Now look, you're going to Frencham tomorrow. You'll spend the whole of Christmas shuttling between an empty cottage and your grandfather's hospital bed. At least have a night out first.'

'I wouldn't enjoy it,' protested Lyall.

'You don't have to enjoy it. Just make the effort to go.'

'No, I . . .'

'Are you trying to make me feel badly, too?' Mitch demanded.

Lyall looked up, her slanting green eyes startled. 'Of course not. I don't know what you mean . . .'

'Well, you met Paul through me.'

Defeated, as much by her friend's genuine concern for her as by the attempt at emotional blackmail, Lyall pushed back her dark, silky hair and agreed, 'All right, I'll go.'

'Wear your green dress,' instructed Mitch, wasting no time now she'd achieved her object. 'It makes you look like one of those water nymphs.'

'Downright wet?' Lyall suggested with a touch of her old humour.

'That's more like it.' The other girl didn't bother to hide her relief. 'Now do something with your hair and face. David's picking us up at eight-thirty sharp.'

David was Mitch's boyfriend, a gangling, fair young man with chocolate-brown eyes and a spiky sense of humour. He was an engineer, working for a small firm which specialised in electronic switchgear and control apparatus. He had a pleasant, friendly disposition, but though Lyall liked him very much she felt no urge to play gooseberry.

'I'd sooner go separately,' she demurred.

'Oh, no, you don't,' Mitch said flatly. 'You might feel tempted to sneak off home as soon as I took my eyes off you.'

Lyall sighed and gave in. When her flatmate was in one of these moods, she tackled any opposition much as a terrier tackles a rat.

Her spirits at zero, Lyall got ready. Paul, young as he was, had been on the executive staff at Jameson's and he should have been taking her to this party. But Paul was dead. Still, for Mitch's sake, she must make an effort not to spoil the evening.

When she emerged from her bedroom, Mitch surveyed her critically, 'That hairstyle's all right for work, but it's no good for a party.' Advancing on Lyall, she pulled some wisps of hair free from the neat coil to curl in soft tendrils around the pale oval face. 'There, that's better! But you still need something. Where's that choker with the green stones?'

Colour came and went in Lyall's cheeks. She'd been forced to sell the necklace along with most of her other pieces of jewellery. The agent who had managed to find her the ground-floor flat in Marylebone she needed so desperately for when her grandfather came out of hospital had demanded three months' rent in advance.

Seeing the telltale flush, Mitch said quickly, 'The jade ear-rings, then.'

'No, I couldn't wear those.' Lyall's voice shook. The ear-rings had been Paul's last gift. When she'd protested, as she had done many times before, that he shouldn't spend his money on her, he had grinned and said, 'They're an advance Christmas present.' Now Christmas was here and Paul wasn't.

Mitch rushed away, to return after a moment holding a pair of antique pearl ear-drops. 'Here, these will do fine. I don't wear them since I've had my ears pierced.'

Knowing it was useless to argue, Lyall obediently fastened the silver screws to her small lobes.

Herself clad in a blue satin harem-pants outfit, Mitch stood back to inspect her handiwork. The chiffon dress, in subtle shades of green and grey, emphasised the slim, dark-haired girl's fragile, almost ethereal beauty, while the ear-rings and wispy curls softened the chignon's stark simplicity. Satisfied at last, Mitch went to answer the door to David's ring, saying over her shoulder, 'Now try to sparkle.'

'I'll try,' Lyall promised meekly.

'Hi,' David greeted her cheerily. Then he gave an enthusiastic wolf-whistle. 'You'll wow 'em in that! There won't be a man in the place who isn't bowled over!'

'There'd better be *one*,' Mitch told him darkly.

The party was in full swing when they arrived on the third floor of Montana House, the imposing modern building which housed Jameson's offices. A large lounge area, its focal point a tall silver tree, was sparkling with tinsel and decorations, noisy with voices and laughter and beat music.

All Lyall wanted to do was weep but, with that inner strength she'd inherited from her grandmother, she did her best to join in the festive gaiety.

She was standing on the edge of a talking, laughing

group of Mitch's friends and colleagues, mentally isolated, but with a bright mask in place, when she happened to glance up. Across the sea of heads she found a brilliant gaze fixed on her. A faint smile of satisfaction touched the man's firm mouth, almost as if he'd *willed* her to look.

His eyes never leaving hers, he crossed the room—a lean, wide-shouldered, powerful man, dark and sophisticated in impeccable evening clothes, yet with a kind of raw, primitive maleness. He seemed to tower over her five feet five, and, suddenly unaccountably breathless, she waited, expecting some sort of opening gambit before he asked her to dance.

He smiled down at her, gold-flecked hazel eyes gleaming between thick lashes, and said softly, 'Let's get out of here.' Putting a hand beneath her elbow, he began to shoulder a way to the door, pausing only to allow her to collect her silver-grey fun-fur jacket from the rail.

Afterwards it amazed her that, as if under a spell, she'd let him take charge of her without a word of protest.

He led her into the lift and touched a button. His hair was thick and peat-dark, curling a little around the neat scroll work of his ears and into the nape of his neck. Lyall was studying his face, the high forehead and level brows, the way his heavy-lidded eyes tilted slightly upwards at the outer corners, the cleft in his square chin, when, with a shock of surprise, she registered that they were going up, not down, as she'd subconsciously expected.

Sharply she asked, 'Where are you taking me?'

'To the penthouse for some supper.' He spoke as casually as if they had known each other for years.

She shook her head and repeated what Mitch had told her some weeks earlier. 'The penthouse belongs to Mr

Jameson, and he's in the States.'

'No, he's not,' her companion contradicted.

Startled green eyes lifted to his face. '*You're* Mr Jameson?'

'Jordan,' he said, as they stepped out of the lift into the quiet luxury of the penthouse foyer. Slipping the pale fur from her shoulders he handed it to a middle-aged manservant, who had silently appeared, and led her through to a striking lounge.

The whole of one wall was sliding glass panels which looked out on to a roof-garden where concealed lighting lit the evergreen shrubs and trees surrounding a paved patio. A faint splash and gurgle came from a marble basin where a slender, graceful nymph poured water from an overflowing pitcher.

All the furnishings were tasteful and deceptively simple, the colour scheme maize and white. Complementing the central heating, a log fire blazed in an iron cradle standing in a wide stone hearth. A black leather couch and some comfortable-looking chairs were grouped in front of it and, a little to one side, an oval candlelit table was set for two. The lights were low, an ice-bucket held a bottle of champagne, and soft music completed the classic seduction scene.

Lyall's somewhat dazed eyes returned to the tall figure of her host, to find he was studying her intently.

'What will you have to drink?' he asked smoothly.

She shook her head. 'I think there's been some mistake.'

'Oh?'

Making a small, nervous movement, she said stiffly, 'Well, obviously you were expecting someone who . . . who didn't come.'

'Oh, but she did.'

'You can't mean me!'

'Can't I?' His tawny glance teased her.

'Look, Mr Jameson . . .'

'Jordan.'

Ignoring the interruption, she ploughed on, 'You can't be serious. You don't know my name or anything about me. You've never even seen me before tonight, so you can't possibly have been expecting me.'

'Wrong on all counts.' He took her chin and, thumb and fingers spread, held her face up to his.

She stood as if frozen.

Looking down at her, he said, 'You're Lyall Summers. You're twenty-two years old and single. For the past year you've been working for Dunn's, a small specialist firm of valuers and auctioneers. You share a flat with Miss Mitchell, from Accounts. I saw you for the first time three days ago when you met her here to have lunch together. I *was* expecting you. And I *am* serious.'

Bewildered, Lyall picked on one point. 'You *couldn't* have been expecting me! I didn't intend to come to the party.'

He smiled, a white, slightly crooked smile that crinkled his eyes and filled his face with such devastating charm that Lyall's heart gave an odd lurch. 'I arranged for Miss Mitchell to persuade you.'

'But why?' she asked helplessly. 'I don't understand.'

The hand holding her chin gentled, and his thumb stroking along her jawline sent a shiver through her. He studied the perfect bone structure of her face, the long-lashed almond-shaped eyes, the lovely curve of her mouth, and said softly, 'You're quite exquisite.'

Alarmed by the gleam in his eyes, she backed away,

pulling free of his hand.

He shook his head. 'I've no intention of seducing you, Lyall.'

'I've no intention of letting you.' She tried hard to sound cool and self-possessed.

'So we're in agreement.' He went to a miniature bar set in one corner of the room and turned, his look a challenge. 'Now, what will you have to drink?'

Lyall hesitated, torn between a wish to run for safety and an out-of-character temptation to play with fire. And if she stayed, that was what it would be. Despite his avowal, she was sure he was dangerous. But she would look a fool if she bolted like a frightened rabbit. Besides, she felt a burning curiosity to know why Jordan Jameson had gone to this amount of trouble, just what his intentions were.

'Dry martini?' he suggested with a lift of one dark brow.

She swallowed. 'Please.'

Having selected two glasses, he poured gin and dry vermouth, adding ice and a twist of lemon.

'You can relax,' he told her mockingly as he handed her a glass. 'I'm not planning to get you drunk or molest you in any way.'

'Just what *are* you planning?' Lyall asked with a boldness she was far from feeling.

'A quiet supper with a beautiful companion.'

'Why pick on me? You must know lots of beautiful women.'

His lips twisted. 'Beauty isn't as common as you seem to imagine. In any case, I'm rather out of touch. I've been in the States for the past six months. I only got back to England the day I first saw you.' His glance moved over her once more, taking in the slender curves, the delicate bones, the grace that was evident even in stillness. 'Next morning I asked Miss Mitchell about you.'

A frown creased Lyall's smooth brow. 'She didn't mention it.'

'I asked her not to.'

'Why?'

'I wanted to surprise you.' He smiled a little.

His mouth was beautiful, with a very masculine beauty and a disturbing sensuality. She found herself staring at it, unable to drag her eyes away.

'Are you ready to eat?'

She jumped at the soft question, and coloured as she realised he had noted her absorption. 'Yes, I . . . I'm not very hungry, though.'

'Well, do your best. We don't want to hurt Wilkes's feelings.' He was laughing at her.

Taking the glass from her nerveless fingers, he seated her at the table.

Suddenly, silently, like the genie from the lamp, the manservant appeared with wedges of pâté, and toast wrapped in a spotless white napkin.

As if under a spell, Lyall began the meal. But, even as she tried not to look at Jordan, her eyes were drawn irresistibly to his.

'Any special man in your life?' he asked lightly.

'No.' A giant hand tightened on her heart.

'Brothers and sisters?'

'I'm an only child.'

He leaned forward to fill her glass with champagne. 'Parents?'

'I never knew them.' In answer to his lifted brow, she continued baldly. 'They weren't married. My father was killed riding his motorcycle six months before I was born. He was nineteen. My mother was seventeen. She died having me. My grandparents brought me up.' Lyall's face grew tender with warmth and a lingering sadness. 'They were marvellous to me.'

'Where do they live?'

'In Frencham. But there's only Grandad left. Gran was killed when a lorry went out of control on the hill and ploughed into a bus queue.' Somehow she kept her voice steady. 'Several other people were injured, Grandad among them.'

Jordan's handsome eyes, amber in the candlelight, narrowed. 'When was that?'

'Three months ago.' Lyall swallowed. 'He was on the critical list for days. His condition had only just started to improve when they were forced to tell him about Gran. The shock brought on a heart attack.' She stopped and, to hide her emotion, bent her dark silky head over the salmon steak which had been placed before her.

It had been a terrible time. Lyall felt sure that, at first, her grandfather had wanted to die, too. But stubbornly she had willed him to live, scarcely daring to leave his bedside, afraid, if she relaxed her vigil, he would slip away. Only when he was well on the road to recovery had she left Frencham and returned to the flat in Buckton Place and her job.

Pulling herself together she drank some champagne from the narrow, fluted glass and said levelly, 'He's much better now, though he's still not discharged. I go down to see him as often as I can.'

'Without a car it can't be an easy journey,' Jordan remarked. 'Wouldn't it be better to stay there?'

'Frencham's only a small country town and there aren't any jobs.' It was that very lack of opportunity which had driven her to the city in the first place.

He moved to refill her glass, and firelight flickered across his face, turning the high cheekbones to Indian bronze. 'And it's necessary to have a job?'

'Of course.' She was puzzled by his question. Did he imagine she came from a wealthy background? If so, nothing could be further from the truth. Flatly she said, 'Until the accident, Grandad was head gardener at Leyton Hall. He's lived all his life in a small tied cottage.'

Jordan surprised her by saying, 'Mine did much the same until he borrowed enough capital to start an electrical engineering firm in an old barn. Now Jameson's is a multi-million-dollar Anglo-American concern, and still expanding.'

Lyall found herself murmuring one of her grandad's pet sayings. 'Tall oaks from little acorns grow.'

'Very true,' Jordan agreed blandly.

The soft-footed manservant removed the used plates, brought a delicious-looking Pavlova and a tray of coffee, and put fresh logs on the fire before asking, 'Will there be anything else, sir?'

'Nothing else tonight, Wilkes.'

Lyall's fingers tightened around the stem of her glass. She'd felt comparatively safe while they were being waited on. Jordan had kept his distance, making no move to touch her or even allow his knee to brush against hers beneath the table. But now . . .

As the servant, tall, thin, first cousin to the invisible man, moved away, Jordan said *sotto voce*, 'Don't look so alarmed.

Wilkes has his own quarters in the penthouse. He's sure to hear if you scream.'

Knowing he was baiting her, she replied with determined lightness, 'Ah, but will he *come*?'

'If he does I'll fire him,' threatened Jordan, his tone as light as her own.

When they had done justice to the sweet, he indicated the coffee-pot. 'Will you pour?'

'How do you like it?'

'Black, no sugar.'

While she filled the dainty, gold-rimmed cups, Jordan crossed to the stereo and changed the tape. Then, at his suggestion, they moved to the couch to drink their coffee.

It was warm and intimate in the flickering firelight. A log settled, sending up a shower of bright sparks. The haunting love music from *Tristan and Isolde* began to weave a poignant spell.

Lyall glanced up to find Jordan's eyes fixed on her, a strange expression in their brilliant depths. Alarm bells began to sound in her head. Abruptly she straightened and asked over-brightly, 'Won't you tell me about the States?'

'Of course.' His tone was dry. 'How could I refuse such an eager request?'

Colour came into her face and she looked down, her thick lashes flickering against her cheeks. It wasn't long, however, before she forgot her embarrassment and relaxed, well entertained by his always amusing, often cynical, account of the American way of life.

Eventually a faint musical chime drew her eyes to the ormolu clock. 'Oh,' she exclaimed, 'it's twelve already!'

'Christmas Eve,' Jordan agreed.

'I didn't realise it was so late. I ought to go.'

'What's the hurry?' he enquired lazily. 'The night's still young.'

'But I came with Mitch and David.'

'I'm aware of that, but they won't wait for you. I told Miss Mitchell I would be taking you home.'

How sure he'd been! 'Then please take me now,' Lyall said with determination. 'I need to catch a bus at eight-thirty in the morning.'

'To where?' he asked.

'I'm going to Frencham to spend Christmas with my grandfather.'

'Don't you drive? Wouldn't it be easier to hire a car?'

'I do drive, but it's too . . . I prefer to go by bus rather than hire a car.' She'd just stopped herself admitting that hiring a car was too expensive for her tight budget.

Running lean fingers over his chin, Jordan said, 'I thought your grandfather was still in hospital.'

'He is, but it's a small hospital and the staff are very good. They'll let me stay with him during the afternoon and evening.'

'Where will you spend your nights?'

'At Grandad's cottage.'

Jordan raised one level brow. 'Alone?'

'Yes.'

'An empty cottage doesn't seem much of a place to enjoy Christmas.'

'I wouldn't . . .' Lyall broke off. She couldn't say she wouldn't enjoy Christmas wherever she was, because he might ask why, and she didn't want to talk about Paul. Hastily she changed it to, 'I wouldn't want to be anywhere else.'

'You must be very fond of your grandfather.'

'I am.' All the love she felt for the sick old man shone in her green eyes. 'He's all I've got left.'

'And vice versa, I presume?' As she nodded, Jordan rose to his feet with easy grace. 'Then we'd better make sure you're not late tomorrow.' He led her through to the foyer and put her jacket around her shoulders.

The lift took them smoothly down to the large underground car park. In a matter of minutes Lyall had been helped into the silver-grey Jaguar in Jordan's private bay, the sleek car had climbed the ramp, and they were slipping through the midnight streets.

It had been a strange, exciting, disturbing evening, Lyall thought. She still had no real idea what had prompted Jordan Jameson's actions . . .

Without asking directions or making any attempt at polite conversation, he drove to Buckton Place. When the car drew up under a lamp in front of the ugly square building where the girls had a modest second-floor flat, he got out and came round to open Lyall's door.

The air was crisp and cold, the moon, seen through the moving clouds, ringed by a halo of frost. A few large flakes of snow were drifting gently down. 'An angel's passing by,' Lyall murmured to herself. Then, at Jordan's questioning glance, she gave him her lovely, luminous smile and explained, 'When I was a little girl, my grandmother always used to tell me that snowflakes were really feathers from an angel's wings.'

He smiled back. 'Mine used to say that stars were the lamps of heaven and each angel had one to tend. While they did their jobs well the lamps burnt brightly in a clear sky. But if they forgot to trim the wicks, the lamps smoked and you couldn't see the sky for clouds.'

Laughing, Lyall added, 'And if some young, nervous apprentice angel dropped his lamp, that was a shooting star.'

'I can see our grandmothers had a lot in common,' Jordan said gravely.

He was standing quite close gazing down at her, and all at once she felt a strange, breathless excitement begin to heat her blood. No man had ever had such an overpowering effect on her before. Becoming aware that she was standing there like someone mesmerised, she blurted out, 'Well, thank you for supper.'

'My pleasure,' he assured her. 'I'll see you at nine o'clock tomorrow . . . no, *this* morning.'

'But I'm going to Frencham,' she protested.

'I know. I'm driving you there.'

While surprise kept her rooted to the spot, the door closed and the car purred away.

The flat was dark and empty, but Lyall felt unable to just go to bed and sleep. The excitement Jordan had generated had banished her weariness and left her restless. She was making herself some coffee when the outer door banged, and a moment later she heard footsteps on the stairs and a key in the lock.

Mitch came in alone. 'Coffee!' she exclaimed. 'Just what I could do with. But what are you doing back? I thought you'd be later than this.' She yawned widely. 'I need my bed. We've another party tomorrow night; that's why David's gone straight home. But first hurry up and tell me what happened tonight.'

'Why didn't you say anything?' asked Lyall reproachfully.

'He asked me not to. And I thought if you knew you

might dig your toes in and not go,' Mitch admitted. 'But, now you've met him, don't you think he's the most gorgeous hunk of man?'

When Lyall didn't immediately answer, Mitch demanded, 'Surely you like him?'

'I'm not sure,' Lyall said doubtfully. The word 'like' was far too tame to apply to someone as disturbing as Jordan.

'There's not a woman at Jameson's who wouldn't give her all to be in your shoes. Are you seeing him again?'

'He says he's driving me to Frencham tomorrow. Though I don't know why he should.'

'You must have bowled him over.' Mitch put a dramatic hand on her heart. 'Love at first sight.'

Lyall shook her head. 'He didn't give me that impression.'

'Probably because he's a sophisticated man he can hide it better than most. And what other explanation could there be? Did he try anything?'

'No.'

Mitch sighed. 'That was the one thing that worried me. I wondered how you'd cope with a man like that if he really turned on the heat. From what I heard of his reputation before he left for the States, he's a real smooth operator. No woman he fancied stood a chance. Not that I can imagine any of them wanting to.' She rolled her eyes. 'But if he didn't try the fast seduction bit, he *must* have fallen for you.'

CHAPTER TWO

'HE's here!' announced Mitch excitedly, a bright morning sun turning her fluffy blonde curls into a halo as she peered from the window.

It was barely nine o'clock, but Lyall was waiting, dressed in a beige and white wool skirt and matching jacket. Her weekend case was standing beside a holdall stuffed with books and magazines, some pipe tobacco, and various small luxuries she had collected for her grandfather. She gathered up her light mac and shoulder-bag, and the two girls gave each other an affectionate hug.

'Watch your step,' Mitch warned, a mother hen with her chick.

Lyall shook her head. 'If he didn't make a pass last night . . .'

'He might have held off to lull you into a false sense of security.' Mitch appeared to have abandoned her original theory. 'Still, I can't see how he can get up to much between here and Frencham. Not in broad daylight, anyway.'

Lyall laughed and picked up her luggage. 'Have a good Christmas. Give my regards to David's parents.'

Though he had a flat in town, David always went to his parents' home in Hampshire for Christmas, and this year Mitch was going with him. David's entire family, from as far apart as Cornwall and Scotland, always gathered together to celebrate the birth of Christ.

Apparently it was a joyful and happy reunion, a once-yearly explosion of goodwill and merriment, reinforcing family ties. 'And making us jolly glad we live apart for the rest of the year,' David had remarked with cheery cynicism.

As Lyall reached the top of the stairs, Jordan appeared at the bottom. He was casually dressed in dark trousers and a cream polo-neck sweater, an olive-green jacket swinging from his wide shoulders. He took the uncarpeted steps two at a time, light and agile for so large a man, and relieved her of everything but her shoulder-bag.

Sitting in the cushioned comfort of the Jaguar's front passenger seat, Lyall studied him surreptitiously. Jordan's dark profile was clear cut and excitingly masculine, the nose straight, the bone structure strong. Though too rugged, with that firm jaw and cleft chin, to be conventionally handsome, it was one of the most attractive faces she had ever seen. The kind of face, with its touch of arrogance, which turned most female heads.

She wondered afresh why he had chosen to drive her to Frencham. Whatever his motives were, it had saved her a long and difficult journey by bus, and she should be grateful. She *was* grateful. A shade primly, she said as much.

'But you doubt my motives?' His voice was clear and cultured, without affectation, a warmly pleasing voice. Now it held a teasing note.

'Yes,' she admitted, startled by his thought-reading.

'You don't put it down to altruism?'

'Should I?'

'You can decide that when you know me better.'

It seemed he intended to further the acquaintance. Lyall felt a flutter of mingled apprehension and exhilaration.

'You did say there was no special man in your life,' he pointed out, as if countering her unspoken misgivings.

But it had been the difference in their backgrounds which had worried Lyall. Carefully she said, 'We come from dissimilar worlds.'

'Our grandparents didn't,' he objected. 'And I was brought up in the country, so I can't believe our childhood was so very different. Didn't you have an apple-tree swing?'

'Yes, I did.' She chuckled. 'I fell off it so many times that Gran read Grandad the riot act for putting it up. I can still remember the smell of the witchhazel Gran used to dab on my bruises.'

In response to his interest she found herself telling him everything he wanted to know about her life, her family, her friends. The only person she couldn't bring herself to talk about was Paul. The shock and grief of his death were still too new, too raw.

The journey was comfortable, leisurely, and Lyall felt, if not happy, at least as close to being happy as it was possible to be; more alive than she'd felt for weeks.

When they reached a pretty little hamlet, where creeper-covered cottages and a thatched inn nestled and slept like contented babes around a village green and duckpond, Jordan stopped the car. He parked beneath some skeletal trees, the black tracery of branches stark against a sky of cornflower blue, and asked, 'Would you like to take a walk before we have lunch?'

Suddenly embarrassed by the unusual way she'd talked and talked, she nodded and said quickly, 'Yes, that would be lovely.'

'Will the shoes stand it?' He glanced at her neatly shod feet.

'Oh, yes.' Her tan leather court shoes had a reasonable heel and wouldn't sink into the frozen ground.

It was a wonderful day for walking. The sun, shining with more enthusiasm than warmth, made the chilly air like sparkling wine. Jordan climbed a stile, then offered a hand to help her over. She took it and felt the shock of his touch make every nerve in her body sing into life.

'You feel cold,' he observed, and, when she would have withdrawn her hand, kept it in his and, in an intimate gesture which quickened her pulse rate alarmingly, returned them both to the warmth of his pocket.

In companionable silence they walked for about a mile, following a track through the bleached countryside, before Jordan glanced at his thin gold watch and suggested, 'We'd better be getting back.'

They had an excellent lunch at the Punchbowl Inn and afterwards fed a dabble of ducks with filched rolls before continuing on their way.

When they arrived at the cottage hospital, Jordan said easily, 'I'd like to meet your grandfather,' and accompanied Lyall inside.

A plump, cheerful nurse led them to a small side-ward. 'He'll be pleased to have some company,' she assured them. 'The other two patients were fit enough to go home for Christmas, so he's on his own at present.'

At the far end of the cream-painted ward, Joe Summers was slumped in a chair by the window looking out over the neatly kept grounds. He was a nice-looking man with broad cheekbones and a high forehead over which his grizzled hair fell in a cowlick. Though turned sixty, before the accident he had been tanned and fit, well built and active. Now he was pale and gaunt, an old man crippled and bereft, his face lined, his eyes defeated. But they lit up at the sight of Lyall.

'Hello, love.' She stooped to kiss him fondly, before explaining that Jordan had driven her down, and introducing the two men.

'Jameson ...' Joe repeated. 'Anything to do with Jameson's Electronics?'

Jordan grinned. 'Got it in one.'

Joe grinned back. 'So Lyall's flatmate works for you ...'

Jordan treated the older man with a totally unexpected deference, while her grandfather, Lyall soon discovered, was delighted to have someone like Jordan to talk to.

She had thought it unlikely that the quiet country gardener and the jet-setting businessman would have anything in common, but there she was proved wrong. Both enjoyed the country and liked animals, both were well read and shared a similar taste in music, and both, it transpired, had a passion for chess.

'Do you play?' Jordan asked Lyall.

'Yes, but not well enough to make a good opponent.'

As she sat listening to the men talk, Lyall felt proud of her grandfather. Joe had done manual work all his life because he enjoyed it, but he'd had a sound education, and even now boasted an active mind and a keen intelligence.

He was able to appreciate the finer points of the electronics industry and thoroughly enjoy Jordan's dry and often caustic wit; while Jordan listened to his tales of country lore and the various animals he had kept, with obvious enjoyment.

'When I was a boy I had a bulldog,' Jordan said

reminiscently. 'I called him Dracula.'

'Because of his fangs?' Lyall asked, diverted.

'He was old when he was given to me,' Jordan told her. 'He hadn't many teeth left, and what he had got were loose. Mother had to mince his food. But until the day he died he terrorised all our callers.' The two men exchanged glances.

Distrusting Jordan's gravity, Lyall objected, 'He couldn't have had much of a bite.'

'No, but he had a very nasty suck.'

Joe laughed heartily at Lyall's indignant look. 'You fell for that one, my girl, and it's one of the oldest in the book.'

He was laughing, actually laughing! Oh, thank God. It was as if some invisible barrier had been broken down.

The doctor had tried to explain Joe's lack of progress by saying, 'If he *wanted* to get better, that would make all the difference.' And surely the ability to laugh again was the first hurdle taken?

Around four o'clock a pretty young nurse brought an urn of tea, some thin bread and butter, and a plate of yellow slab cake. She went into a complete dither when Jordan smiled at her, and almost dropped the cup and saucer she was holding.

Evening started to spin a grey dusk and the lights were switched on, but still Jordan showed no sign of leaving. It was after six-thirty and the patients' evening meal was being served before Lyall turned to him and suggested hesitantly, 'Don't you want to be getting back to town?'

His eyes, gleaming topaz in the yellowy light, met hers. 'I'm in no hurry. I thought I'd stay and take you out to dinner.'

'Good idea,' Joe said instantly. 'And don't think of coming back here tonight. They get us settled down early.

There'll be no waiting up for Santa.' He grinned, the gap between his two front teeth giving him, even now, a little-boy look.

He had all his own teeth still and, when outdoors, had usually held a pipe clenched between them, his light blue eyes half closed against the spiralling smoke. The Matron of Glendale, an understanding, compassionate woman, allowed a morning and evening smoke.

As Lyall smiled, overjoyed that he felt up to making even a feeble joke, Jordan said smoothly, 'Then we'll see you tomorrow. I'll give you a game of chess.'

When they were out of earshot, Lyall asked exasperatedly, 'Why did you tell him you'd see him tomorrow and play chess? Now he'll be looking forward to it.'

'And he won't be disappointed. You don't think I'm going to go back to town and leave you to spend the night alone, do you?'

They had left the antiseptic warmth of the hospital and were walking towards the car park. Shivering in the cold air, Lyall said angrily, 'If you imagine for one moment that I . . .'

'I don't imagine anything,' he broke in calmly. 'I've decided to book us both into a hotel. Separate rooms, of course,' he added.

Determinedly ignoring the mockery, she said, 'I've no intention whatsoever of booking into a hotel. I'm going to stay at the cottage.'

'Then I'll stay there with you.'

'You will not!' she retorted with spirit.

He shrugged slightly. 'The choice is yours. Either you join me or I join you.'

'You can't stay at the cottage. Grandad won't be able to

go back there.' For a moment her voice wavered dangerously. 'And everything's gone except for a couch and a few things in the kitchen.'

'So a hotel it is.'

Reluctantly Lyall told him the truth. 'I can't afford to stay at a hotel.'

'I'll be happy to take care of the bill.'

She stopped abruptly and turned to face him. 'I wouldn't dream of letting you pay my bill!'

They were within the radius of a lamp and she saw a frown draw his dark brows together before he said adamantly, 'And I wouldn't dream of letting you stay alone in an isolated cottage.'

'I really don't see what makes it any of your business.'

Ignoring her fury, he attacked from a different angle. 'Doesn't the thought of it worry your grandfather?'

Brought up short, Lyall bit her lip. There was no denying it *was* worrying him. When he had discovered she meant to stay at the cottage, he'd done his utmost to talk her out of it.

Rose Cottage *was* isolated—though how Jordan had known that was a mystery—but when Lyall had stayed there previously the neighbouring cottage had been occupied. Now that, too, was standing empty, the owner, William Leyton of Leyton Hall, having at last decided to have them both modernised.

'Well, doesn't it?' Jordan applied pressure.

'Yes,' she admitted, honesty forbidding her to lie about it.

'Surely in his state he shouldn't have any worries?'

Jordan had won the battle and they both knew it.

Casually he said, 'You get in the car and I'll go back and tell him, set his mind at rest.'

After a few minutes he returned and slid into the driving seat with an air of satisfaction.

'I shall be paying my own bill,' Lyall told him firmly.

He slanted a glance at her. 'Very well.'

It was about a mile to the small market town, and he chose a modest family hotel in the centre, watching her reaction with a sardonic gleam in his eye.

Lyall said nothing, well aware that it wasn't his style and he'd only settled for Greyfriars because of her insistence on paying her way. But on that she was determined. He *might* have altruistic motives, but there was no way she was going to be in his debt.

It proved impossible to keep that vow, however. Next morning, when Lyall assembled her grandfather's small pile of gaily wrapped presents, Jordan insisted on adding a beautiful, and clearly expensive, pocket chess set which had been in the glove compartment of the car. He didn't give her anything, and for that she was thankful, having nothing for him.

Despite the shadow of Paul's death, Christmas proved to be much happier than Lyall had ever anticipated. The hotel was clean and comfortable, with good food and a friendly atmosphere.

Jordan showed no inclination to return to town, and both mornings, after breakfast, they went for a walk before spending the afternoon and evening with Joe.

By the time they left late on Boxing Day, her grandfather looked a new man, and Lyall knew she had Jordan to thank for that. She'd done all she could, given all she had to give, but Jordan had been able to supply new interest, a fresh incentive.

After they had stopped on the way for a leisurely dinner

at a hotel, it was quite late when they got back to Buckton Place. Seeing no lights, Lyall guessed Mitch hadn't yet returned from her visit to David's family.

Over the three days, Jordan had behaved impeccably. He had made no attempt to touch her or even flirt with her. Yet Lyall was never quite at ease when they were alone. Perhaps it was her own reaction to him that gave her this sensation of walking a tightrope, she thought. It would be only too easy to fall for him, and affairs weren't in her line.

And surely that was what he was leading up to, be it ever so gentle an approach? Even if he had just returned from the States, she couldn't believe he was so devoid of social life as to make spending most of his Christmas sitting in a hospital a welcome prospect. Unless he had some ulterior motive . . .

But whatever his motives or his feelings, he was far too disturbing, too potentially dangerous, for her peace of mind. She was too aware of him, too affected by his magnetism. She had worked hard to appear cool and self-possessed, but her defences were about as impregnable as glass armour, and she was loath to invite him into an empty flat.

Carrying her case, he followed her up the stairs and waited while she took out her key. Turning to him, she said carefully, 'You've been more than kind. I don't know how to thank you.'

'You could ask me in for a coffee.'

Flustered, she sought for an excuse. 'Mitch has been away, so there'll be no milk.'

Jordan refused to accept his dismissal. 'Then it's a good thing I take my coffee black.'

Of course he did. She could have kicked herself. 'Well, I . . .'

'You'll be quite safe,' he told her caustically. 'My primitive urges are well under control.'

Scarlet-cheeked, avoiding his eyes, Lyall handed him the key. He unlocked the door and with a mocking flourish held it open for her.

The air in the living-room was cold, and she stooped to switch on the electric fire before going through to the cramped kitchen. Rattled that he had forced her hand, Lyall made no attempt to get out the percolator. Let him make do with instant!

When she returned he was standing at ease, his back to the fire. She handed him one of the mugs of coffee and stood to drink her own, her attitude making it plain she was waiting for him to leave.

While he drank he prowled around the comfortable, shabby room, stopping in front of the lop-sided bookcase, where everything slid to the left, to examine its contents. 'Who do the books belong to?'

'They're mine. Mitch isn't much of a reader.'

Jordan glanced along the top shelf, where a volume of John Donne's poems and a Mills & Boon romance were sandwiched between *The Wind in the Willows* and *I Capture the Castle.* 'I see you have catholic tastes,' he remarked with a touch of amusement.

'I enjoy almost anything that's well written.' She was annoyed with herself for sounding defensive.

Putting down his mug, Jordan picked up the John Donne and began to turn the pages. Something about his absorbed expression, the way his long, sensitive fingers handled the book, made her ask, 'Do you like poetry?' Silly question, she chided herself silently. He probably thought poetry was only for women or effeminate types.

But he was answering, 'I've always enjoyed poetry. I can get carried away by words. Have you ever read any of Michael Childer's?'

Lyall shook her head and admitted, 'I've never heard of him.'

'He's a little-known modern poet, with so far a couple of volumes to his credit. He writes about things rather than people, and the way he uses words is very evocative. One of his poems, which describes a snow scene encapsulated in an old paperweight, I find particularly fascinating.' Jordan replaced the book he was holding and added politely, 'Thank you for the coffee.'

Remembering his kindness to her grandfather, Lyall suddenly felt ashamed of the way she'd treated him. Taking a step towards him, she said, 'Before you go, I would like to thank you for . . .'

'There's no need for thanks,' he broke in.

'But there is.' Lyall lifted grave green eyes to his face. 'You were so good to Grandad.' Seeing a slight twist to his lips, she added in a small voice, 'And to me. I don't understand why you went to so much trouble.'

'I wanted to.'

'But why?'

'Because I intend to marry you.' Jordan spoke so casually that she doubted her own hearing.

Her voice squeaking a little, she asked, 'What did you say?'

'I want to marry you.'

She stared at him in confusion. He didn't look as if he was

joking. 'We've only just met,' she protested. 'You scarcely know me!'

'I know all I need to know,' he assured her softly.

'But I hardly know you at all.' She tried to speak calmly, reasonably.

'I'm sure that can be remedied. Start by having dinner with me tomorrow evening?'

He gave her a smile which turned her legs to water and her blood to champagne, and she found herself stammering. 'Thank you . . . I'd like to.'

'Good.' Turning towards the door, he said over his shoulder, 'Then I'll pick you up at seven.'

If leaving so abruptly was a tactical move on his part, it was a successful one. Lyall felt a sudden disappointment that he had made no effort to touch or kiss her, or even just stayed to talk.

From then on he took her out most evenings, and at weekends they went down to Frencham. As she got to know Jordan better she discovered the tough outer shell was only part of the real man. Though he had a crusader's passion for justice, he could be kind, compassionate, and generous to a fault. He had an appreciation of nature, a love of order and beauty, and a sensitivity she hadn't suspected.

He brought her flowers and chocolates, and courted her with a charming, old-fashioned propriety she had never expected a man like him to display, and which she found almost irresistible. Though he didn't mention marriage again, his attentions—and intentions—were so obvious, his attitude so proprietorial, that Joe smiled knowingly, more than happy with the way things were going.

Mitch was equally delighted and didn't hesitate to say as much. 'You lucky so-and-so! He's just fabulous!' then, darkly, 'I'd have you bumped off if I thought that with you out of the way he'd look at little old me.'

Lyall only smiled, knowing full well that Mitch adored her open, easy-to-understand David, and would be right out of her depth with someone as complex as Jordan.

The following Tuesday was Joe's birthday. Lyall asked for the day off work and Jordan took her down to Frencham to be with him. On the way back to London they stopped at the quaint old Lamb and Flag Inn for an early evening bar snack. The place was, as yet, only half-full and they had no difficulty finding a secluded table.

Jordan leaned back, a pint of lager in his hand, his long legs stretched idly, clearly enjoying the inn's rustic charm.

'You puzzle me,' Lyall remarked.

He raised a dark brow. 'Oh, in what way?'

She struggled to put the thought into words. 'Well, you seem such a . . . a city man, yet you always look at home in the country.'

'I *am* at home in the country, but I enjoy town life too.'

'Which appeals to you most?'

He grinned boyishly and admitted, 'Wherever I happen to be. I have a capacity for enjoying what's there at any particular time. When I'm at business I enjoy it, nothing else exists. When I'm not, who cares about work? Life's for living here and now, not for saving until tomorrow.'

Lyall smiled and said, 'I can only admire that philosophy. I think in some ways I share it, at least the "present mirth hath present laughter" bit.'

When they were ready to leave, Jordan rose to put her fun-fur jacket around her shoulders. It slipped through his fingers and fell to the floor.

As he stooped to pick it up she said jokingly, 'Mind my mink!'

'Would you like a mink?' he asked, his dark face suddenly intent. 'I can give you anything you want—clothes, furs, jewels . . .'

She shook her head dumbly.

Over the past weeks, apart from an increasing pleasure in his company, Lyall had felt a growing rapport, a harmony, between them. Now his words were so out of tune with what she was feeling that abruptly it was shattered.

As if sensing he had said the wrong thing, Jordan let the matter drop.

The flat was in darkness when they reached it and, anxious to dispel the faint cloud hanging over their relationship, she suggested coffee. While they sat in front of the fire drinking it, he asked. 'How much better will your grandfather get? Will he walk again?'

Lyall shook her head and, having had time to come to terms with it, answered levelly, 'The hospital doctor told me he'd be confined to a wheelchair for the rest of his life.'

'What about his heart?'

'They say he'll be all right so long as he's spared shocks or stress of any kind.'

'I understand he should be well enough to be discharged in a month's time. What had you planned to do then?'

'I've managed to rent a small ground-floor flat about half a mile from here. It comes vacant at the end of February. It's not ideal—there are some steps, and not all the doors are wide enough to take a wheelchair—but it's the best I can do.'

'Won't your grandfather mind living in London?'

'I was worried about that,' she admitted. 'But he says he

won't. And if I'm to keep my job we haven't much option.'

'How will he cope if you're out at work all day?'

It was a question she had asked herself more than once. She sighed. 'I don't know. But we'll manage somehow. We have to.'

'If you marry me you won't have to "manage". I'll take care of everything.'

Lyall's throat tightened. 'If you mean put him in a home . . .'

'I don't mean anything of the kind,' Jordan said. 'It would be enough to kill a man like that.'

'Then what do you mean?'

'You want him with you, don't you?'

'Of course I do.'

'In that case, he can live with us. You can give him your company, and for the rest I'll engage a nurse. I can also arrange for some private treatment to ease any pain and possibly make him more mobile.'

'Oh, Jordan,' was all she could say, her green eyes swimming with tears of thankfulness.

'So will you marry me, if only for your grandfather's sake?' There was a strange note in his voice.

It wasn't the way she had dreamt of being proposed to. Far from being an 'anything goes' girl, beneath her outward air of sophistication she was simple and old-fashioned, romantic as they come. She wanted to be loved and needed by the man of her choice, but this sounded more like some business deal. Herself in exchange for what he could give her. If not clothes, or furs, or jewels, then her grandfather's comfort.

'Well, Lyall?'

Just those two words kicked her previous theory out of

the window. They held an almost painful intensity, a barely suppressed excitement that convinced her this was no cool business deal. The answer really mattered to him.

'Yes,' she breathed, 'I'll marry you.' She wanted to tell him that it wasn't for her grandfather's sake. For Joe she would have done almost anything, scrubbed floors, worked her fingers to the proverbial bone, yet not even for him could she have married a man she didn't love. But, tongue-tied by a kind of shyness, and the knowledge that Jordan had tried to conceal his feelings, she couldn't find the words.

It had taken her until now to admit it even to herself but she knew it had begun that very first evening. In spite of being out of his class, in spite of her initial distrust, in spite of everything, she loved him with a depth of passion she hadn't known she was capable of.

Though his relief was evident, Jordan made no move to kiss her. She waited for what seemed an age before taking a tentative step towards him and lifting her face in mute invitation.

He took her in his arms then and kissed her with a cool expertise that seemed to bear little relation to love, or even desire. But after a moment the coolness vanished and, one hand on the softness of her nape, the other spread across her spine, pressing her against him, he kissed her with a hungry passion that made her body melt and her head reel. When he finally let her go she staggered a little, and he had to put out a steadying hand.

'If we get married a week on Friday . . .'

'A week on Friday!' she gasped. 'Oh, but couldn't we wait until Grandad's out of hospital?'

Drawing her back into his arms, Jordan rubbed his cheek against hers and asked huskily, 'Do you really want to wait?'

Lyall wriggled a little, as the roughness of his cheek against hers sent shivers of pleasure through her, and admitted breathlessly, 'No, I don't. But I would like him to be at our wedding.'

Jordan's lips moved to caress her ear before brushing lightly across her mouth. 'Let that date stand and I'll see what I can arrange.' He punctuated his words with tantalising baby kisses. 'If we get married then we'll be able to have a honeymoon and be home for when Joe is finally discharged. Shall we go down tomorrow evening and tell him?'

'Mmm,' she agreed as his growing ardour made further words seem unimportant.

Lost in a world of sensual delight, Lyall would have been unable to lift a finger to prevent him if he'd taken her to bed. But after a while he drew away and said ruefully, 'If I don't leave this very minute we'll end up shocking Miss Mitchell!' He dropped a light kiss on her nose, murmured, 'See you tomorrow,' and was gone before she could collect herself enough to say goodnight.

When Lyall went to bed she lay awake for quite a time gazing into the darkness. Warm waves of happiness kept washing over her, while her body remembered with delight the touch of Jordan's hands, and longed for more.

Next morning Lyall was still sound asleep when a banging on her bedroom door and Mitch's voice calling, 'Aren't you going to work today?' roused her.

Only half-awake, she stumbled out of bed and into the bathroom to brush her teeth and take a hasty shower. She was in the kitchen in her old blue woolly dressing-gown, gulping down a cup of coffee, when the blonde girl burst in practically gibbering with excitement. 'He's here! He says he's taking you out to choose an engagement ring.'

'Taking me to choose a ring?' Lyall put a hand to her head. 'But I'm supposed to be working.'

'Don't let that stop you,' Mitch advised crisply. 'But, you sly thing, why didn't you tell me?'

'It only happened last night.'

'I could see it coming, of course,' Mitch said smugly. Then, apparently taking in Lyall's dazed state, 'Come on, hurry up, don't keep him waiting. He's out there looking eager as a boy!'

Lyall doubted that. Though Jordan was a man of strong emotions, they were always kept under tight control.

She dressed, did her hair as quickly as possible, and hastened into the living-room. He rose to his feet with a smile but made no move to kiss her, and she guessed it was because Mitch was there. In a lot of ways he was a very private person.

'Ready to go?' he asked.

'Yes, I . . . I suppose so. But the shops won't be open yet.'

Unperturbed, he said, 'I've rung Peter Gresham. He's expecting us. I thought if we made an early start you needn't be too late for work. That is, if you want to go in today?'

For once in her life Lyall didn't want to, but she answered, 'I feel I should.' Mr Dunn had been good enough to give her the previous day off, so she didn't want to let him down. And she ought to hand in her notice straight away, to give him as much time as possible to find a replacement.

As they crawled through the morning snarl-up of traffic Jordan suddenly asked, 'What do you think of as the ideal marriage, Lyall?'

She saw the ideal marriage as a partnership, two people

linked together by love and emotional ties, but standing separately, each able to support the other with their own kind of strength when the need arose. She said as much.

He looked momentarily startled, as if it hadn't been the answer he'd expected, and she wondered if he would prefer to have a weak, pliant woman who would cling to his male strength like decorative ivy.

Jordan wasn't an easy man to get to know and understand. At times she'd caught him looking at her as if he found her enchanting, at others there had been a cool, withdrawn expression on his rugged face, as if he wanted to keep her at arm's length. Perhaps, if he really had fallen for her, he resented the fact a little. Loving someone gave them power over you. Power to hurt you.

Gresham's was a small unpretentious jewellers in a quiet street in Mayfair. Peter Gresham, a fair, well dressed man in his forties, was waiting for them. After murmuring a greeting he led them through to a private room at the rear of the shop and from a large safe produced several trays of rings.

They were all magnificent, and Lyall stared at them, her wits scattered, her heart beating fast, quite unable to choose. After a minute or so, her cheeks flushed, she gave Jordan a beseeching glance.

He selected a diamond solitaire and asked, 'What about this?' Taking her left hand, he slipped it on to her third finger.

It was a perfect fit. She caught her breath at the beauty of the huge, sparkling stone.

'Like it?' Jordan asked.

She hesitated, knowing it must cost a fortune, then said tremulously, 'It's lovely, but I . . .'

Jordan gave Peter Gresham an almost imperceptible nod.

'A fine choice, if I may say so,' the jeweller remarked as he replaced the trays of rings in the safe. He accepted Jordan's cheque and handed him a leather ring-case.

When Lyall would have removed the solitaire, Jordan stopped her. 'I'd like you to wear it.' In an undertone he added, 'I want to feel you belong to me.'

His words and the possessive look in his eyes made her tremble. His arm around her slim waist, she left the shop wishing everyone in the world could be as happy as she was. Only one thing could possibly have made her happier. If Jordan had whispered that he loved her.

CHAPTER THREE

LYALL sat in the front seat of the Jaguar and, sighing, stretched slim ankles gratefully beneath the flow of warm air. Apart from other traffic, the only sounds were the shush of tyres, a smooth purr from the powerful engine, and the faint swish of busy wiper-blades.

The lights were coming on as Jordan, with silent concentration, deftly eased the car through the Friday homegoing bustle. She looked at him, longing to touch him, to run her fingertips down his cheek, to trace the shape of his mouth and the cleft in his chin.

Apparently conscious of her scrutiny, he glanced at her. Eager to establish some contact, some closeness, she smiled at him. For once he didn't answer her smile, and his hazel eyes, as they swept over her, held a strange glitter. She shivered, and he looked away.

Gazing at London's darkening streets through an arc the wipers kept clear, Lyall watched the snow falling. Odd gusts of wind scurried it along, making the homegoing pedestrians bend their heads against the driving white curtain.

Street lamps, hovering, luminous ghosts, shed pools of light, catching the feathery flakes in the glare like motes swimming in the beam of a spotlight. It was snowing faster now, drifting and eddying, decking the great metropolis in bridal white.

Bridal white. Somehow she had always imagined she

would have a white wedding. She'd visualised herself walking up the aisle on Joe's arm, a conventional bride, to a handsome, blond, blue-eyed bridegroom, while Gran, bless her, sat in the front pew in a flowery hat and cried buckets of tears.

Nothing could have been further from the reality. Jordan, though handsome, was no blue-eyed boy, Gran was no longer here, and the ceremony had been a civil one. But, with the power that money can buy, Jordan had arranged for her grandfather to be transferred from the cottage hospital to a private convalescent home in London. He had been brought in his wheelchair to the register office, and was now on his way back to the home.

When they returned from the Lakes he would be coming to live with them in the penthouse. At first it had seemed odd, a handicapped person living in a penthouse, but on reflection it made sense. The rooms were all on one level, there was the extensive roof-garden, and a lift straight up from the car park.

Everything that Jordan had planned had gone smoothly. She ought to be relaxed and happy, but somehow she wasn't.

From beneath her long, curly lashes she stole another look at him. She knew his everyday likes and dislikes, his taste in books and music, his dry humour, the side of himself he had chosen to show her. But there was an inner reserve that she'd never managed to penetrate. Though he was her husband now, in some ways he was still a stranger. Another shiver ran through her.

'Are you cold?' he asked.

'No.' She managed a smile. 'It's just someone walking over my grave.'

There was no comforting word, no reassuring touch. Lyall looked at the lean hands lying lightly on the wheel, long, well shaped hands with neatly trimmed nails, the muscular wrists dark against the immaculate white cuffs. The thought of those hands caressing her made her stomach tighten into a knot.

On the little finger of his right hand he was wearing a heavy gold signet ring. She would have liked to exchange wedding rings, but Jordan had said nothing and, for some reason she couldn't fathom, she had hesitated to suggest it. Now she wished she had. If he'd been wearing her ring it might have made a difference.

It wasn't easy to clarify her thoughts, but somehow she felt she now belonged to him without the reverse being true.

Don't be a fool, she chided herself silently. But, since hugging Mitch and her grandfather and leaving the register office after the brief, dry-as-ashes ceremony, she had felt a growing unease. Jordan had been silent and aloof, a look on his face, in his amber eyes, not of happiness, but of . . . triumph?

Her nerves rippled like the surface of a pool when a chill breeze blows over it. Though it had been his masculine arrogance that had first attracted her, previously it had been softened by the warmth of his charm. She had never seen him in quite this sort of mood before and didn't know how to deal with it. But she'd learn.

Goodness knew, she hadn't wanted a mamby-pamby man, but like most women she had hoped for a man who would give her love and tenderness and understanding. Jordan was capable of all these, she was sure, even if at the moment he was exhibiting none of them.

Warm now, she slipped the grey suede gloves from her

slender, fine-boned hands, and her eyes were drawn to the chased gold ring that sat snugly beneath her solitaire. It wasn't the narrow, dainty band she had envisaged, but a wide, ornate *fetter*. The word sprang to mind unbidden. She tried to push it away. It had a connotation she didn't want to think about.

Jordan had chosen her wedding-ring; she hadn't even seen it until he had slid it on to her finger. As soon as she had accepted his proposal he'd forged ahead swiftly with the wedding arrangements, almost as if he couldn't wait to make her his wife, so surely he must love her. She clung to this thought.

Snow was falling faster now as they left London behind them and took the M1 north. Lyall had been surprised by Jordan's choice of a Lake District cottage for their honeymoon. She had half expected he would take her abroad, perhaps teach her to ski, but when he had told her his plans she'd been happy to agree.

The thought of being alone with him, and the knowledge that he had wanted to be alone with her, had filled her with a heady excitement, the kind of excitement he had generated from their very first meeting. She imagined them eating an intimate meal in front of a blazing log fire, sharing a chair while they sipped their coffee, then afterwards . . . She quivered at the thought. When Jordan touched her it was like setting a match to dry straw.

None of her previous boyfriends had managed to raise her temperature one iota, yet when Jordan took her in his arms and kissed her, fire raced through her veins and her body burnt for him.

Always reserved about her innermost feelings, Lyall had never spoken of it. But Mitch had guessed. At the thought of her friend's outspoken comments, Lyall smiled.

'Aren't you the lucky one!' the blonde girl had said. 'I bet he makes a fabulous lover. All that lusty male passion . . . What wouldn't I give to find someone like him in my maidenly bed!' She had raised her eyes to heaven as though in prayer.

'His mouth sends shivers right down my spine. So does that masterful look . . . But my guess is he'll be tender and romantic with the woman he loves.' She sighed. 'You'll get the best of both worlds.'

'Do you really think he loves me?' Lyall had asked eagerly.

'Loves you?' Mitch had snorted inelegantly. 'You must be joking! He can't take his eyes off you. Anyone can see the poor fool's besotted!'

But even now, even after going through a marriage ceremony with him, Lyall still had doubts. All she knew was that she'd fallen for him like someone leaving a plane at ten thousand feet without a parachute.

As they headed north the weather worsened, but it was pleasantly warm in the car, the rhythm of the wipers soporific, and gradually Lyall slipped into a doze. She awoke to find they were at a service station, drawn up before a row of squat petrol pumps. 'Whereabouts are we?' she asked.

'Half-way up the M6.' Jordan sounded remote. 'Would you like a drink while we're here?'

'Yes, please, I'd love one.'

The petrol paid for, he drove to the car park and, slamming his own door, came round to open hers. Snow was falling fast, driven by a bleak wind, and their feet crunched on the crisp white layer.

Clad only in the lilac wool suit she had bought for the wedding, Lyall shivered. She would have like to snuggle in the protection of Jordan's arm, but he strode beside her without so much as a glance.

There was only a scattering of cars in the parking area and a few heavy goods vehicles to their left. On a strip of snowy grass, just within range of the lights, a solitary figure was walking a shaggy black dog.

The steamy cafeteria smelt of stale smoke and fried onions. It was empty except for a balding businessman gulping down a cup of tea, and one or two lorry drivers reading evening papers as they ate their way through platefuls of sausages and greasy chips.

'Coffee?' Jordan asked.

'Please.' They were polite and distant as two strangers.

Presiding over the drinks section was a mature, heavily made-up blonde, wearing a pink nylon overall. Her vapid expression changed to one of fascinated interest at the sight of Lyall's companion. She darted the younger woman a quick, envious glance before returning her gaze to Jordan.

'Nasty night,' she remarked. When he failed to answer, she went on, 'Shouldn't be surprised if we were snowed up by morning. The last time it came down like this I didn't get home for two days.'

Still Jordan said nothing, and Lyall murmured with a smile, 'Well, let's hope it's not so bad this time.'

The coffee was hot and surprisingly good. Jordan swallowed his rapidly and, when Lyall glanced at him, asked, 'Ready?'

She nodded and, putting down her half-empty cup, led the way to the door. Jordan opened it and, a hand beneath her elbow, hurried her through the swirling snow to the car. She had been oddly reluctant to leave the garish warmth of the cafeteria. What on earth was the matter with her? Lyall wondered unhappily as she slid into the Jaguar and brushed snow from her shoulders. The answer came swiftly. It was the change in Jordan. Now it was too late, had he had second thoughts?

He got in beside her and put the key in the ignition.

'Jordan . . .' She touched his arm, her fingers slim and pale against the charcoal sleeve of his formal jacket. 'You don't regret marrying me?' The words tumbled out in a rush.

Turning his head, he looked at her. Her dark, silky hair was spangled with snowflakes, her beautiful green eyes unconsciously pleading.

'Why do you ask?'

Lyall twisted her wedding ring round and round her finger. 'Because you suddenly seem to dislike me,' was what she wanted to say. But surely she was being ridiculous? Letting this strange mood make her imagine things? 'I . . . I just wondered,' she murmured lamely.

'No, I don't regret it,' he said emphatically and, starting the engine, joined the slip road back to the motorway.

She gave a little sigh. There was no doubt he'd been speaking the truth but, even more than a denial, she'd been longing for a smile, the touch of his hand, some sign that he loved her.

She glanced at him. His dark profile was grim and set. The weather had worsened rapidly and it was now blowing a full-scale blizzard with gusts of wind that rocked the car. Visibility was down to a matter of yards and traffic speed had been reduced considerably. A white shroud covered the road surface, and the wipers had a job to keep the windscreen clear.

'How much further?' asked Lyall.

'We come off at the the next junction.'

If conditions were this bad on the motorway, surely they would be even worse on ordinary roads? Her supposition proved correct, and when they struck across country the journey became a nightmare.

'Perhaps we'd be better stopping at a hotel?' she suggested. He didn't answer, and intuition told her he had no intention of giving up his plan to reach the cottage that night.

They passed a deserted garage, half smothered beneath the relentless white force, a pub, its sign swinging wildly, then beyond, their windows gleaming with yellow lamplight, a straggling row of cottages. A mile or so further on they took a left turn, the nearside wheels hit a drift and the car slewed alarmingly. Jordan eased back on the power, fighting to keep control. For a few seconds the wheels spun uselessly before getting a grip.

Conditions had become well nigh impossible when welcoming lights shone out cheerfully through the snow, and they drew up in front of a long, low building set back from the road.

'This is it,' said Jordan with satisfaction. 'Drum Cottage.'

Lyall breathed a sigh of relief, eased the tension from her cramped limbs, and picked up her handbag.

'Wait here a minute,' Jordan ordered crisply. Fighting against the elements, he took their luggage from the boot and, unlocking the cottage door, thrust their cases inside before coming back for her.

Once out of the car, buffeted and half blinded, Lyall had

a problem keeping her feet. With his arm tightly around her, their heads bent against the icy wind and driving snow, they struggled the few yards to the door and up the shallow steps.

The blizzard practically blew them in, whirling snowflakes around them like confetti. Turning, Jordan forced the door to and dropped the latch. The storm shut out, it suddenly seemed quiet. They shook off the loose snow, stamping their feet on the doormat that lay across the entrance.

The interior was open-plan, the front door opening straight into a large, attractive lounge area. The walls were white, the ceiling criss-crossed with oak beams in an unusual diamond pattern. A chintz-covered settee and two armchairs, with an oblong coffee-table between them, were grouped in front of a big stone fireplace in which glowed the dying embers of a fire.

On each side of the fireplace were recessed shelves, holding books, a television, and a stereo. A dark refectory table with matching chairs and a sideboard made up the rest of the furniture. Several radiators provided background heat, and sheepskin rugs were scattered on the gleaming parquet floor.

Beyond the lounge was a kitchen, screened by a fancy stone lattice which formed the back of a breakfast bar. To the left, four polished steps led up to a bedroom area. There was a vanity unit set between built-in wardrobes, and a large divan bed with a cabinet each side. The tangerine duvet matched the curtains. A door in the end wall was ajar, showing a flash of oyster tiles.

Just the short trip from the car had chilled and wet Lyall's feet. She crossed to the fireplace and, slipping off her grey suede courtshoes, held each slim foot to the warmth in turn. Conscious that Jordan was studying her, she broke the silence to say, 'It's a lovely place. Who does it belong to?'

'Some friends of mine.' His firm lips twisted. 'They were delighted to lend it to me when I explained that it was for my honeymoon, and I didn't want to stay anywhere as public as a hotel.'

Something in his tone made her strangely uneasy. She swallowed. 'Who lit the fire and turned on the lights?'

'Mrs Smith from the village. She should also have stocked the fridge and the freezer. She's paid to come in a couple of times a week and make sure the cottage is aired. She offered to come in daily while we were here and tidy up for us, but I told her we wouldn't want to be disturbed.'

The words should have sounded romantic, but instead they held a faint hint of menace, as if concealing some kind of threat.

Oh, really, Lyall thought crossly, she was behaving like an utter fool. She'd heard of bridal nerves, but this was beyond all reason! Drawing a steadying breath, she said, 'Then you've been here before?'

'I came up one day last week to make sure the place was suitable.'

'Oh.' She wondered why he hadn't mentioned it.

While Jordan stirred the whitish ash and carefully piled logs on to the embers, Lyall went in her stockinged feet to explore further.

The bathroom, she saw at once, was a woman's choice. There were several full-length mirrors, and a long, mirrored cabinet ran along one wall holding a selection of bath oils and toilet requisites. Everything looked new and luxurious. Soft towels hung on a heated rail between a sunken bath and a shower cabinet in oyster pearl. It looked so tempting that Lyall wanted to indulge there and then. But she ought to see about a meal. She was a wife now, and after the long and difficult journey Jordan must be tired and hungry.

The kitchen was nicely designed and fitted. As well as a conventional electric oven it had an infra-red grill and a microwave. Above the stainless steel sink unit, primrose and white curtains were drawn across the window.

On the end wall, an alcove held a stock of dry logs. Next to it, a white-painted door, with bolts top and bottom, opened into a pantry-cum-storeroom. Well-stocked shelves ran the length of one wall, while low on the other a kind of flat cupboard housed a panel of fuse-boxes. The bolts were presumably because of an unguarded window at the far end.

The back door had a heavy, full-length glass panel with a white ornate metal grille, and Lyall could see the snow piling up against the outside of the glass. It looked as if they were going to need Mrs Smith's supplies.

Only yesterday she would have been thrilled and excited at the thought of being snowed up here with Jordan. Now a strange, nameless apprehension made her skin gooseflesh.

Giving herself a shake, she opened the cupboards and fridge and surveyed their contents. A tin of soup would do to start, followed by steak, with rice and a dish of mixed vegetables. They could finish with cheese and fruit.

Taking off her suit jacket, Lyall donned a yellow apron she found in one of the drawers and began to prepare the simple meal. As she worked she gradually relaxed, and was humming softly to herself when she glanced up to see Jordan leaning against the breakfast bar, his tawny eyes fixed on her.

Abruptly her nerves tightened. His attitude put her in mind of a cat watching a mouse. She pushed the thought firmly away and gave him a little smile. 'Nearly ready.' While she set their places at the table he produced a bottle of Nuits St Georges and some long-stemmed glasses from the sideboard.

The lobster bisque, with a pinch of tarragon and a swirl of cream, was delicious; the rice was white and fluffy; the vegetables colourful and fresh-tasting; the steak, served with a mouth watering mushroom sauce, was seasoned and grilled to perfection.

After a couple of forkfuls, Jordan asked in surprise, 'When did you learn to cook like this?'

'I've cooked all my life,' she told him. 'Gran taught me. In her younger days she was cook at Leyton Hall.'

The meal over, she cleared the table and plugged in the percolator. Apart from Jordan's remark and her reply, they had eaten in silence. Glancing at him, she'd seen that his lean, strong face was remote, his brilliant eyes shuttered, and strands of her previous tension had returned to tie her tongue.

When she brought in the tray of coffee, he had switched off the overhead lights, leaving only the standard lamps still burning, and was sitting in his shirt sleeves, staring broodingly into the fire.

Lyall filled two cups and handed one to him, then on an impulse took her own and sat on the rug at his feet, her shoulder against his knees. The only sounds were the distant howling of the gale, and the crackle and rustle of the logs in the grate.

Head tilted back a little, she gazed into the flames, heavy lashes drooping almost on her cheeks, her lovely face, the exposed throat, vulnerable in the firelight. When Jordan made love to her she would forget the silly fancies that had plagued her. Though she was inexperienced, she could show him by her response how very much she loved him. And surely, when the barriers were down, he would admit that he loved her. Her face soft and glowing with dreams, she sighed.

His hand slid under her chin, tilting her head back on to his knees, and as he bent to kiss her she caught a glimpse of his dark face intriguingly inverted before her eyes closed . . .

Lyall stirred and opened her eyes to find daylight filtering through the curtains. She turned her head, but the pillow beside hers was empty. A glance at her watch showed her it was almost twelve, but she still felt dazed with sleep and there was a dull ache behind her eyes. Not exactly the picture of a radiant new bride, she thought ruefully.

With a sigh she let her thought drift back to the previous night. For some reason sleep had deserted her and for a long time she had lain wide awake, listening to Jordan's quiet breathing.

As Mitch had forecast, he had proved to be a wonderful lover. But, in spite of that, Lyall knew herself to be disappointed. She had been ready and eager for him, but the actual moment of possession had been painful and she had been unable to prevent a little cry, an involuntary movement of rejection. Jordan had stilled, his whole body going rigid.

'It's all right,' she'd whispered, stroking his cheek. 'It's all right.'

Perhaps the knowledge that he'd hurt her had thrown

him because, though he had gone on to give her the greatest physical pleasure, something had been missing. She had always thought the act of love should be a spiritual as well as a physical union, a coming together of hearts and souls and minds, as well as bodies. Somehow they hadn't achieved that closeness. The knowledge made her sad.

Pushing herself up on one elbow, she looked around. The living-room curtains had been opened and a fire blazed merrily in the grate, but there was no sign of Jordan. Lyall got out of bed, her naked body, slender and pale, goosefleshing in the slightly chill air, and made her way into the bathroom.

She brushed her teeth and showered, then, wrapped in one of the big, fluffy towels, rooted in her case to find fresh undies and a moss-green jumper and skirt. The rest of her unpacking could wait until after lunch. She dressed, leaving her hair loose, then, pausing only to draw aside the bedroom curtains, went into the kitchen.

There was still no sign of Jordan and he didn't appear to have had any breakfast. Lyall peered through the window to find the blizzard had blown itself out, but snowflakes were still drifting down from a leaden sky. The overnight snow lay crisp and deep, piling up against the dry-stone walls and weighing down the green arms of the pine. Marring the white perfection, recent tracks crossed the garden and disappeared through a gap in the wall and into the encircling wood.

Did Jordan usually take a morning walk whatever the weather, or was it some new restlessness that had driven him out into the snow?

With a small frown drawing her well marked brows together, Lyall set the table and, while rashers of bacon sizzled beneath the grill, poured water into the percolator and plugged it in. The appetising aroma of coffee was starting to fill the kitchen when a movement outside told her Jordan was back.

She broke eggs into the frying pan and flicked fat over them knowing, from those few days in the hotel, that Jordan liked his bacon crispy and his eggs with their eyes closed but the yolks still runny.

As she slid them on to a hot serving dish the door opened, letting in a gust of icy air. Jordan stooped to pull off his wellingtons, banging them together to get rid of the clinging snow, before closing the door and removing his sheepskin jacket.

He was wearing brown trousers and a cream roll-neck sweater, and his dark hair was damp and curling into his neck. She smiled at him, and was dismayed to get only a cool glance in return.

A sick feeling growing in the pit of her stomach, she said as brightly as possible, 'Lunch is ready.'

'Practising being a dutiful wife?' His words sounded like a sneer.

Trying not to show the hurt, she asked, 'Don't you want a dutiful wife?'

He took his place at the table without answering. She poured coffee for them both and sipped hers while Jordan ate silently. When he had finished he rose, still without a word, and went to sit in front of the fire.

Lyall cleared away, washed the few dishes, then, determined to have it out with him, went and took a seat opposite. He was staring into the flames, his dark face morose.

'Jordan,' she said quietly, 'what's wrong?'

He looked up, a strange gleam in his gold-flecked eyes. 'Wrong? What could be wrong?'

Lyall bit her lip and struggled with sudden tears. His whole attitude declared that something was very wrong. She'd just got herself in hand and was preparing to return to the attack when he asked abruptly, 'Tell me, do you ever think about Paul?'

CHAPTER FOUR

'PAUL?' The name was a shocked whisper.

'Yes, Paul. Paul Heyton.'

'I . . . I didn't realise you knew Paul.'

'Apart from the fact that he worked for me, he was also my foster-brother.'

'Your foster-brother?' Lyall gaped at him. 'But he didn't even mention knowing you . . . And Mitch never said anything.'

'She wouldn't be aware of any connection. I brought Paul into the firm to do some undercover work for me. A couple of our best ideas had been leaked, and I suspected industrial espionage.

'When I had to go to the States, I needed a man I could trust implicitly to keep an eye on things for me. We thought it would give Paul an advantage if our relationship was kept secret.'

'He didn't so much as hint . . . I thought he had no family.'

'I'm sure you did,' Jordan agreed grimly.

Lyall looked at him blankly, uncomprehendingly.

Jumping to his feet, he began to pace the room like a caged tiger.

After a moment she got up and went to him. 'Jordan, why did you never mention Paul?' She put a hesitant hand on his sleeve. 'I don't understand why you've waited until now to . . .'

He brushed her hand away as if he hated her touch. 'I had my reasons. Why did *you* never mention Paul?'

'Because I . . . Well, his death had been such a shock and I . . . I couldn't bring myself to talk about him.'

'Conscience pricking you? Surely not!'

'Conscience? I don't know what you mean.'

'You sound so innocent, my dear Lyall, that I could almost believe you if I didn't know what an excellent actress you are.'

'I don't know what you mean,' she said again.

'I mean the way you played hard to get. Your "reluctance" to marry me. You almost managed to convince me it was genuine. Whereas the only thing you were honest about was making sure your grandfather was going to be taken care of.

'Suppose I'd insisted on putting him in a home? What then, Lyall? How far would your love and loyalty have stretched? Would you really have turned down the chance to be a rich man's wife?'

Her throat feeling as if it was full of hot shards of glass, she denied, 'I didn't marry you for your money, if that's what you think.'

He laughed harshly. 'I don't think. I *know*. You made it clear from the very first night that you didn't want just an affair. But, for curiosity's sake, if I hadn't stated my intentions, and instead started buying you expensive presents, would you have changed your mind and settled for what you could get? Or, having, as you thought, caught a really big fish in your net, stuck out for wedding bells and hoped to get a substantial pay-off when I discovered what kind of woman I'd married?'

'You must be mad!' she choked. 'You talk about me

catching you, but it was you who made all the running. You didn't *have* to marry me . . . And, as you're thinking like this, I can't understand why you did.'

'Have you forgotten Paul?' His voice cracked like a whip.

'Paul? What has Paul got to do with it?'

'Everything. Haven't you heard of retribution?'

'R-retribution?' she stammered. 'Retribution for what?'

'For what you did to Paul.'

Lyall was shaking her head helplessly. 'I don't . . . I don't understand what you mean.'

'Then I'll spell it out for you. He was mad about you, completely besotted. You took him for every penny he had. When the supply of money stopped and he began to get desperate you just turned the screw. That's when he started drinking heavily. If he hadn't been drunk out of his mind he'd have been able to unfasten his seatbelt in time to save himself being burnt alive.'

Lyall covered her face with her hands, pressing her fingers hard against her eyes, trying to shut out the awful picture his words evoked. But it was still there inside her head.

'You're responsible for his death,' Jordan accused.

'No, oh, no . . .' she moaned. But hadn't he put into words the feeling of guilt that had lurked like a black shadow at the back of her mind?

He pulled her hands down. 'You've an alluring body and a lovely face, a look of radiant innocence that's quite breathtaking. If I hadn't known what you were really like you might have bewitched me just as you bewitched Paul.

He loved you to distraction, and you pretended to love him while it suited you.'

'No, I didn't!' she cried. 'I never pretended anything. You've got it all wrong.'

'So I've got it all wrong, have I? You'll be telling me next that he didn't love you.'

'He d-did say he loved me. But I couldn't help it. I didn't want him to love me.'

'Didn't want him to love you!' Jordan snapped furiously. 'You led him on, wound him around your little finger, used him until he had nothing left to give you!'

Anger overrode every other feeling and she cried, 'I did nothing of the kind! How dare you say such things!'

But he was going on relentlessly, 'You put Paul through hell, but now it's your turn to pay, your turn to find out what hell's like.' He spoke with a kind of raging calm that made her tremble.

Aghast, she whispered, 'So that's why you've looked at me strangely sometimes. All these weeks you've been planning to make me pay for what you believe I did to Paul.'

'Exactly. How much do you think you'll be able to take?'

She stared at him, mute and trembling.

When she didn't answer he went on almost conversationally, 'That's why I came back from the States. That's why I got to know you. My first impulse was to choke the life out of you, but that kind of justice is frowned on. I decided to marry you so I could make you suffer like Paul suffered.'

Her hands and feet were icy, and perspiration dewed her forehead. He meant it. Dear God, he meant it. 'But what you believe isn't true.' She tried to stay calm, to speak levelly. 'I was very fond of Paul. I would never have deliberately hurt him.'

Jordan reached for his jacket and took a letter from the pocket. Unfolding the thin blue airmail paper, he thrust it into her hand.

The handwriting, sprawling, flamboyant, sloping backwards, was undoubtedly Paul's. Lyall read it, her lips moving silently as she strove to take it in:

> 'I love her—God, how I love her. I didn't know it was possible to feel so desperate. I've begged her to marry me, but she refused, and when I went down on my knees to her, she just laughed at me.'

'No. No!' she cried. 'It wasn't like that.'

Jordan put an accusing finger on the words, 'She just laughed at me.'

'It's not true,' she insisted with spirit. 'It's not. I never intended to hurt Paul, truly I didn't. You can't mean to go through with this crazy plan of yours. The marriage can be annulled and . . .'

'Oh, no,' he said softly. 'There are no grounds for an annulment. I made sure of that.'

The letter fluttered from her nerveless fingers as the full horror of the situation became clear. She felt stricken, appalled. Not only didn't he love her but he hadn't even wanted her. He'd only slept with her to make the marriage a real one.

She sank down at the table her hands clenched on the polished surface, and stared blindly into space, her eyes too big for her small, ashen face. She was filled with a terrible desolation, which was threaded through with anger and bitterness at the ruthless way he'd tricked her into this cruel sham of a marriage.

Though perhaps 'tricked' wasn't the right word. He had never once said he loved her, or even wanted her. All he'd said was he would look after Joe. No, she had fooled herself, pulled the wool over her own eyes, because she loved him.

Her face crumpled like a child's. She bent her aching head and, with a small, despairing sound, laid it on her folded arms . . .

When she finally sat up and brushed back a strand of hair from her damp cheek, she found Jordan was watching her. There was a bleak look on his face, and in his eyes.

Unable to stand his scrutiny, Lyall got to her feet and, finding the bottle of aspirin her handbag contained, went through to the kitchen. She ran water into a cup and had just taken off the bottle cap when Jordan came in like a whirlwind, sending her staggering back. The bottle fell and bounced, scattering the round white tablets all over the rush matting.

The bottle remained intact, with a few tablets still in the bottom. Jordan picked it up. 'How many do you want?' He sounded rattled.

Lyall swallowed and her lips moved, but no sound came. He shook out two tablets and put them into her hand. She drank some water and tried to swallow them, but they refused to go down and dissolved bitterly on her tongue.

Jordan stooped and began to carefully gather together the remainder of the tablets. As she watched him it occurred to her to wonder why he'd rushed in. Surely he hadn't imagined she was going to take them all? Going to use that way out of the trap he'd caught her in?

If he had, he'd misjudged her. Though she appeared to be

delicate, even frail, she was stronger than she looked. Tougher both physically and mentally. There was no way she would deliberately take her own life and leave her grandfather alone, or risk what such a shock might do to him.

She thought of the future with a new surge of fear and anxiety. Jordan had used her love for Joe in his bid to get her to marry him, but what would happen to the old man now?

Lyall swayed a little as she stood. Then, making a great effort, she squared her shoulders and walked back to the living-room. She sat down on the settee in front of the blazing fire and tried to think, to make some plans, but her brain refused to function. Her face felt stiff, her eyelids swollen, and her head throbbed remorselessly. She leaned against the high back of the settee and closed her eyes, squeezing them tight as if to try and shut out the pain.

When she awoke it was to find she was lying full-length on the settee, her head on a cushion, a blanket tucked closely around her. The headache had lifted and she felt better. Under her lashes she could see Jordan sitting by the fire, staring into the flames.

Outside it was still snowing, huge feathery flakes swirling in a grey dusk, but in the leaping firelight the cottage was cosy and intimate. The sleep had cleared her brain and she found it easier to think. Things weren't quite as desperate as they'd seemed. Once she could get away from Jordan and be among other people she would be safe; he couldn't force her to go back to him.

But somehow she had to get through the next hours, perhaps even days. Her blood ran cold at the thought. Though if she could stay calm and establish some normality, perhaps she could get him to listen to her, convince him that she'd never meant to hurt Paul. Then he might let her go.

Pushing back the blanket, Lyall sat up and, her voice as level as she could make it, asked, 'What time is it?'

Jordan looked at her, his glance flickering to the small gold watch she wore on a plain black strap.

'It's stopped. I forgot to wind it up last night.' She couldn't help the tremor.

His lips twitched in sardonic amusment. 'I wonder why?'

Painful colour flooded into her face and she looked down at her hands.

'It's just after four,' he added. 'Would you like a drink?'

'Please.' Not looking at him, she swung her feet to the floor and stood up to fold the blanket neatly.

Her mouth felt desert-dry and when he returned with the tea she drank it thirstily.

'Would you like something to eat?' He sounded polite but distant now, like someone saddled with an unwelcome guest.

She shook her head, finding the thought of food nauseating, then asked, 'Are *you* hungry yet?'

'Wifely concern?' he jeered.

It wasn't going to be easy. But then she'd never thought it would be.

Lyall was searching for something innocuous to say to break the lengthening silence when Jordan remarked abruptly, 'So you hadn't slept with Paul.' Almost to himself, he added, 'I was so sure you had.'

'I'd never slept with anyone.' Her tone was flat, without expression. After a moment she asked hesitantly, 'Why were you so sure I'd slept with Paul?'

'In one of his letters he boasted that you'd said he was fantastic in bed.'

After the first jolt Lyall recalled that light-hearted remark. It had been made one Sunday afternoon in late summer. It was a lovely day and Paul had called at the flat to suggest a picnic on the heath.

Mitch had made them all coffee while Lyall finished packing a wicker hamper. 'Why don't you come with us?' she had suggested to the blonde girl.

Shaking her short, fluffy curls, Mitch had refused. 'You know the old adage about three being a crowd? Anyway, I've got it in mind to paint the kitchen.'

'David not around today?' Paul had enquired, sitting on the table swinging one jean-clad leg. He was slightly built, boyishly handsome in a striped bodyshirt, his fair frizzy hair a halo.

Ruefully, Mitch had admitted, 'David is miffed because I wouldn't stay the night at his flat. Honestly, you men imagine you can get us women to jump into bed with you at the drop of a hat!'

Blue eyes dancing, Paul had murmured, 'Well, I've never had any trouble. Except with Lyall,' he had added hastily at her indignant look.

'You mean the others are queuing up?' Mitch had widened her eyes.

He had grinned. 'Modesty forbids me to . . .'

'All right,' Lyall had said, laughing. 'There's no need to sacrifice your modesty. You're fantastic in bed. We believe you.'

'You don't have to take my word for it.' He had leered at her theatrically. 'I can give you a free demonstration.'

'No, thank you,' she had refused firmly. 'The only

demonstration I need is how to fasten the clasp on this dratted hamper.'

Now Lyall looked up and said slowly, because it still hurt to talk about Paul, 'There was a grain of truth in what he wrote.' In response to Jordan's questioning glance, she told him what had happened, keeping her voice steady only with an effort.

When she had finished, Jordan made no comment, apparently accepting her version of what had prompted the remark. But why shouldn't he? He *knew* Paul had twisted the truth. Wearily she pushed back her long dark hair. 'I just don't understand why he told you that.'

'I understand.' Jordan poked the fire savagely before throwing on another log. 'The first time he fell in love he was seventeen. Things were going fine until he brought her home. I never so much as looked at the girl, but she decided she preferred me. Unfortunately, the same thing happened more than once . . .'

No, Lyall thought, it couldn't have been easy for Paul with Jordan on the scene. She could see how any girl would be bowled over by his powerful sexual attraction. How young and green Paul must have appeared beside his foster-brother's dark sophistication.

'. . . Though he never went overboard for any of them like he did for you,' Jordan was going on. 'He wrote pages singing your praises, telling me how beautiful you were. He wanted me to think he'd made it with you. I can see that now. He wanted me to believe he was getting something in return . . .'

Jordan suddenly swung round to look at her, and involuntarily she cringed away from the savage anger and contempt in his gold-flecked eyes. 'But you gave him *nothing* in return for all the money he gave you.'

'He never gave me any money,' she protested. Then, with a touch of hauteur, 'I've never taken money from any man, and I've never been for sale.'

'You were for sale all right, if the price was high enough. But obviously Paul's wasn't.'

'He never gave me any money,' she insisted.

'Don't give me that,' Jordan said bitingly. 'I know how much he was getting through. His cash came from me, remember!'

'I *didn't* take his money,' she told him raggedly. 'I wouldn't have done such a thing.'

'So what *did* you take? Furs? Jewellery?'

The memory of Paul's gifts brought stinging colour to her cheeks. Lifting her chin she admitted, 'He did give me presents. I tried to stop him but he wouldn't listen.'

'You could have stopped him if you'd really wanted to.'

There was a measure of truth in that. But Paul's gifts had been given with so much excitement and anticipation, with such childlike pleasure, that it had seemed like slapping him in the face to refuse them. When she had dug her toes in and tried, he'd been so cast down and miserable that she'd ended up weakly taking them, unable to hurt him.

But it was no use, Lyall thought defeatedly. Jordan would never believe that, not in a million years.

'Try me,' he invited, as if following her train of thought.

She tried, needing to convince him, desperate to end this nightmare. Before she faltered to a stop she knew she'd failed. Recklessly she suggested, 'Try to believe me. It's the truth. And it wasn't as though they were diamonds,' she added defensively.

'Oh?' Jordan queried sharply. 'Are you trying to tell me

that the things he bought you were paste? Costume jewellery?'

'Most of them were.'

'Prove it. Show them to me.'

Her colour deepened. 'I can't,' she admitted in a whisper.

'Why not?'

'Because I . . . I . . .'

'You sold them,' he accused softly. 'You little bitch! With those wide eyes and that butter-wouldn't-melt look you almost had me fooled.' He flexed his fingers as if he was longing to feel them around her slender throat.

Lyall swallowed hard. 'I wouldn't have dreamt of selling Paul's gifts if I hadn't been at my wits' end. But I *had* to have a ground-floor flat for when Grandad came out of hospital, and the agent insisted on having three months' rent in advance.'

'What did you do with the money that was left? Spend it on clothes? Bank it for a rainy day?'

Shaking her head, she protested, 'There wasn't any money left.'

Jordan came to lean over her, his dark face very close, his voice silky with menace. 'One of these days, when the going gets too tough, you'll tell me the truth.'

'That is the truth. It *is*.' At the blaze of fury in his eyes she fell silent, her heart lurching in fear.

He turned and walked away, as if he couldn't trust himself not to strangle her if he stayed.

Lyall shivered. They were so isolated here, and now it was almost night again. She couldn't bear it if he touched her. Silently she fought the choking panic. Then rationalisation brought relief. He didn't even want her. Last night he'd been intent on making the marriage a real one, but now, hating and despising her as he did, he was hardly likely to want to make love to her. Though she shuddered at the euphemism, she felt a bit easier. Still, she must do something. If she just sat here thinking she'd go mad.

Getting to her feet, she switched on the standard lamps and drew the curtains, shutting out the snowy wastes. Jordan had returned with a fresh supply of logs from the kitchen alcove, and was stacking them in the brass box. Lyall spoke to his back. 'I . . . I'm going to shower, then I'll get a meal.'

When he didn't answer she went to open her case. As she made to lift it on to the bed, which had been neatly made, it was taken from her hand and heaved up effortlessly. She started to thank him, but he was already walking away.

The skirt she had slept in was creased, so she selected a dress in blue-grey check. Then, closing her mind to the implications, she put a white nightdress and négligé and a pair of dainty hand-made mules on a chair by the bed. The mules had been a gift from Mitch. When Lyall had expressed her pleasure, the girl had said laconically, 'What can you buy a woman who'll shortly have everything?'

After a hot, scented shower which refreshed her mentally as well as physically, Lyall dressed and combed her hair into its usual sleek coil before continuing to unpack her case.

Her first impulse had been to leave everything she didn't need still packed, but a moment's thought had overruled that idea. Jordan might wonder why, and if she *could* manage to get away she wouldn't be taking a heavy case.

He had already unpacked, casual stuff mostly, but expensive, Lyall noted as she hung up her own things. Though carefully chosen and matched, hers were the cheap, 'off the peg' variety; answer enough to his suspicions that she might have spent Paul's money on clothes. The only things she owned which had cost more were the lilac suit and silk blouse she'd worn for the wedding, and her grandfather had paid for those.

Jordan had opened a bank account for her but, unwilling to spend any of his money before they were married, she hadn't cashed a single cheque.

The last time she had been alone with her grandfather he'd said, 'I've a bit put aside and I'd like you to have it.' Ignoring her protests, he had gone on, 'You'll need some money of your own. There'll be clothes to get, and you'll be wanting to buy Jordan a wedding present . . .'

Her problem had been what to get. She had wanted his gift to be something special, something which would convey all the love she'd never admitted.

Then, just before she was due to leave work, in a sale of rare items she'd found what she wanted. 'It's beautiful,' she'd told Joe. 'And I'm going to get it if I can possibly afford it.'

It had taken every penny she could scrape up, but she had bought the exquisite little paperweight snowstorm. It stood about five inches high on a round black base. Enclosed in the delicate glass dome was a miniature house with a studded door and twisted chimneys. Moving the paperweight caused a snowstorm, and the snowflakes swirling around the house magically gave the illusion that the tiny windows were lighted. The little scene was so serene and enchanted that Lyall had been instantly captivated. She had packed it carefully, wrapped it in dull gold paper, and put it in her case.

Now she stared at the package, tears pricking behind her

eyes. How he would laugh if he saw it! She was about to push it to the back of one of the drawers when Jordan's voice asked, 'Finished?'

She spun round, her hands going behind her back for all the world like a guilty child.

He took the case and tossed it on to the top shelf of one of the wardrobes, alongside his own, then asked mockingly, 'Were you thinking of stabbing me in the back?'

'I . . . I don't know what you mean,' she stammered.

'I thought that might be a knife you're trying to hide.' When she stayed mute he said patiently, 'So what is it?'

She shook her head stubbornly.

'Secrets, Lyall?' He clicked his tongue. 'There should be no secrets between husband and wife.'

He was enjoying baiting her, and she knew it wasn't going to stop until she told him what he wanted to know.

'It was your wedding present,' she admitted stiffly. 'But now it's . . . There's really no point in giving it to you.' Still clutching it, she walked back to the lounge.

Following her, he said purposefully, 'Oh, but I'd like to have it. I'll be interested to see what you chose for me.'

His face cynical, he took the package from her unready fingers and tore off the wrapping. Abruptly his expression changed. For a moment he looked shaken, then his mouth twisted wryly. 'How very clever of you!' The cruel words were like a knife thrust. 'You're even more devious than I thought. Tell me, Lyall, how did you manage to pay for it?'

'I didn't use a penny of your money!' she flared.

'Oh? Whose money did you use?'

Something seemed to die inside her, but at least the pain was gone. She felt cold and empty, curiously numb. In a voice devoid of expression she said, 'I'll see about a meal,' and headed for the kitchen.

Needing to keep occupied, she prepared an elaborate dinner, in between times setting the table with care and adding twin candlesticks with tall, decorative candles she found in the sideboard.

When the meal was almost ready Jordan came to ask, 'Would you care for a drink?'

Lyall closed the oven door and, her face a little flushed from the heat, answered, 'Please. A dry sherry, if there is one.'

While she took off her apron and put the first course on the table, Jordan produced a bottle of chilled Chablis and filled two glasses. He drew Lyall's chair out for her before taking his own seat, then eyeing the candles remarked, 'A nice honeymoon touch.'

Ignoring the taunt, her face cool and composed, she served the creamy fillets of fish. Jordan ate well and complimented her both on the sole Véronique and the chicken Kiev which followed.

Lyall, however, had no appetite. Head bent, lashes making dark sweeps on her high cheekbones, she sipped her wine and made a pretence of eating. The meringue, served with raspberries from the freezer and whipped cream, was crisp and delectable, and she managed to swallow a little of that. Although already a shade light-headed from drinking on an empty stomach, she let Jordan refill her glass.

When she rose to remove the sweet plates, he said, 'You sit down. I'll clear away and get the coffee.'

None too steadily, she made her way to the couch and, leaning back, closed her eyes. She opened them again with a jerk when Jordan put a tray on the small table and sat down beside her. He poured the coffee and handed her a cup.

Made reckless by too much wine, she said, 'You'd better watch it or you'll be making a good husband.'

Unmoved by her gibe, he replied, 'I intend to make an ideal husband—at least in the eyes of the world. But speaking of being an ideal husband, I still haven't given you *your* wedding gift.'

He got up and returned almost immediately carrying a thin black case which he tossed into her lap. When she made no move to touch it, he prompted, 'Open it, Lyall.'

She shook her head. 'Whatever it is, I don't want it.'

'Oh, I think you will when you see it.' Picking up the case, Jordan flicked the catch with his thumbnail.

The necklace lying on the white satin lining was quite exquisite. It was in the form of a trail of vine leaves with bunches of lustrous green grapes. Lyall stared at it stonily.

'"Emeralds to match your eyes" would be the most romantic thing to say. But, as I know you prefer a purely practical approach, then emeralds costing what would be a year's salary to some people.'

Galvanised into action, she closed the case with a snap and almost threw it at him. 'I don't want it!' she cried fiercely. 'I don't want anything from you. As you think what you do, I don't know why you bought it.'

'Don't be foolish,' he chided mildly. 'People are going to want to know what I gave my new bride. And what's your grandfather going to think if you have nothing to show him?'

'I won't wear it,' she said flatly.

'Oh, yes, you will.' His voice held steel. 'You'll wear it to please me. I've ordered a bracelet and ear-rings to match. I intend my wife to have everything money can buy. Other women will envy you.'

'Envy me! That's a laugh,' muttered Lyall bitterly. 'You can keep your money. There's nothing you can buy that I want.'

'Not even your grandfather's comfort?'

'I didn't marry you for Grandad's sake.'

'You know,' said Jordan silkily, 'I could almost believe that.'

'You can believe it. It's the truth.'

'So why did you marry me? Tell me your version.'

'I was fool enough to imagine I loved you.'

He laughed without mirth. 'You must think *I'm* the fool if you expect me to credit that. Women like you don't fall in love. Not unless it's with a bank balance . . . Still, when you've stopped dissembling, my bank balance is big enough to provide all the sparkle in life you really married me for.'

Sick at heart, she whispered, 'I did nothing of the kind. Oh please, Jordan, I know you hate me, but you can't mean to go on with this . . .'

'Oh, but I do, my dear Lyall. You gave Paul months of hell. Surely you don't expect to get off so lightly?'

He reached out to grasp her wrist and pull her on to his lap. Her heart lurched in fear and she sat frozen and mute. Slowly he began to unfasten the small covered buttons on her dress, watching her through narrowed eyes. Her breath caught in her throat, and when his fingers followed the line of her dainty bra to the warm cleft between her breasts, she couldn't prevent a shudder.

Mockingly he asked, 'Don't you like me to touch you any longer?'

'I loathe it,' she said in a stifled whisper.

'Ah . . .' he murmured softly, and too late she realised she'd given him a weapon he would use against her.

But his hand stilled and he suggested, 'In that case perhaps you'd care to take off your own clothes?'

'What?' she breathed.

'Take off your clothes. Unless you want me to take them off for you.'

Lyall sat as if turned to stone, while an inward battle raged. She wanted to tell him to go to hell. But he was so much stronger than she was; if she resisted, it would only end in defeat. Perhaps he wanted her to resist?

Standing up, she removed her dress and slip. As she hesitated he said, 'The undies are very pretty, but I would prefer you without them.'

She wanted to protest, to plead with him, but she knew it was useless. He intended to humiliate her, and begging would only add to that humiliation.

Colour high, fingers like ice, she took off the other dainty scraps, then stood erect, chin raised, arms by her sides, and looked him in the face.

For a moment she thought she saw a gleam of reluctant respect in his tawny eyes, then it was gone. The irises had darkened and his voice was rough with some emotion as he said, 'Your body's as beautiful as your face. If the inside matched, you'd be the loveliest thing any man could ever dream of . . .' Abruptly he broke off, then added derisively, 'But we know it doesn't.'

He got to his feet and, reaching out, took the pins from her hair, letting the dark, silky mass tumble around her shoulders. Then, so suddenly that she gasped, he stooped and lifted her, one arm beneath her shoulders, the other under her knees. He carried her to the bed and, laying her on it quite gently, sat on the edge looking down at her.

Smiling slightly, he slowly, deliberately, touched her, his lean fingers weighing the fullness of her breast, stroking over the dusky nipple, slipping down the curve of her hip to the smooth, satiny skin of her thigh.

Her stomach clenched in rejection, her mind cried out a wordless protest, but she forced herself to lie quite still.

'Aren't you going to struggle?' he asked softly.

'No.' She put all her will-power into keeping her voice steady. 'You want me to struggle. You want an excuse to hurt me.'

'Now that's where you're wrong. I don't need an excuse. I've reason enough.' As she began to tremble he went on, 'But tonight I don't want to hurt you.' His fingers continued to explore. 'I want to satisfy my curiosity. So tonight is an experiment . . .'

CHAPTER FIVE

'AN EXPERIMENT . . .' This time Lyall's voice was far from steady. 'What kind of experiment?'

Jordan smiled a little, deliberately prolonging the suspense before answering, 'Even if you could get all you wanted from your boyfriends without giving anything back, it's still somewhat unusual in this emancipated age for a twenty-two-year-old woman to be a virgin, unless she's frigid.'

His index finger moved to trace the outline of her lips. 'With a mouth like that, and the thought of your response, I find it hard to believe that applies to you. But, then again, it might do. Last night was hardly a fair test. You had to make *some* effort to please your new bridegroom, even if it was only acting.'

Her body jerked as though touched by a live wire as he went on, 'But tonight you don't need to keep up a pretence.'

Lyall stayed still and frozen, her dark hair spread over the pillow. He put a hand each side of her head, trapping the shining strands. She stared up at him, her green eyes enormous, her face making the white pillowcase look as if it had been washed in Brand X.

Gently he mocked, 'What big eyes you've got!'

She lay as if hypnotised, unable to look away. Then all at once her unnatural calm cracked and shattered into a thousand pieces, and she began to struggle, gasping and writhing, hitting out at that lean, mocking face.

Catching hold of her wrists, he held her, using only as much force as was necessary to subdue her. When she finally gave in and lay limp, her heart pounding, her breath being taken into her lungs in great gulps, he released her and began to strip off his own clothes.

In terrible fascination she watched the play of muscle beneath the smooth olive skin, the unhurried grace of his movements, the symmetry which gave that powerful body such outstanding masculine beauty. A strange feeling welled up, like a pain, a hunger, an aching emptiness, a futile longing for what might have been. Then Jordan was beside her, and there was only the here and now.

She had steeled herself, mind and body, against an attack, against masterful hands and hot, passionate kisses. She wasn't prepared for gentleness, for quiet, sweet seduction.

Taking each of her taut fists, he unfolded them, carefully straightening out the fingers one at a time, kissing each one in turn, before bending to brush her lips with his.

Closing her eyes tightly, Lyall willed herself to stay cold and distant. She wouldn't let herself respond. She wouldn't give him that satisfaction.

He laughed softly, as if reading her thoughts, and his mouth started to move sensuously against hers, his tongue coaxing her lips to part. Teeth clenched, she resisted, and his mouth moved away, brushing her creamy throat, travelling across the flawless skin to close gently round the tip of her breast and tug slightly.

She gasped as his lips and teeth and tongue teased the nipple, causing needle-sharp stabs of sensation. His hand moved to her other breast and his fingers and thumb repeated the erotic torment. Her body arched and, desperate to escape his touch, she began to struggle once more. He used his weight to prevent her from thrashing about, while his hands began to move caressingly, stroking, squeezing, probing.

Then his mouth was covering hers again and this time she had no defence against his invasion, his tongue's exploration. By the time he raised his head she was dazed and mindless, on fire, burning with the desire he had so easily aroused.

He moved with slow, deep thrusts until he had built up such an intense core of sensation that she clutched at him convulsively, her nails biting into his back. Even then, despite her incoherent little cries, he took his time, making her wait. Only when she began to move involuntarily against him did he drive for release for them both.

While she lay quivering and languorous, her mind gradually emerged from the mist of physical sensations that had obliterated it. Lifting heavy lids, she saw Jordan was propped on one elbow, watching her.

Softly he said, 'Far from being frigid, there's enough fire beneath the ice to warm a man until he's old.'

Shamed and degraded, she turned away from the gleam in his eyes while like a blow came the knowledge that earlier she had been deluding herself. Jordan might hate and despise her, but he still wanted her.

She recalled clearly one of her colleagues at work, a young divorcee, remarking, 'I get very lonely, especially at nights. I've no lack of offers to share my bed, and quite a few of the men are attractive on a physical level. But I find sex without love is almost unendurable.'

At the time, Lyall had considered that to be something of

an exaggeration. Now she felt it had been an understatement.

Oh, dear God, she thought in despair, what was she going to do? Suppose she got pregnant? She'd once asked Jordan if he wanted children, and he had replied casually that he'd like a family 'sooner or later'. If he had loved her, she would have been more than happy to have had his baby. But this marriage was just a cruel mockery, and the last thing she wanted now was to conceive.

In the circumstances, it was probably the last thing Jordan wanted either, she realised. But, believing her promiscuous, he had no doubt thought she was on the pill. Even knowing she wasn't promiscuous, he might still think she was safely protected. Events had moved so fast, however, that she hadn't even seen her doctor, presuming in her innocence that Jordan would take care of things.

But nothing had turned out as she had expected. Nothing . . .

She was lying awake, engulfed in a misery too great for tears, long after Jordan had turned away and fallen asleep. In the black days following her grandmother's accident and Paul's tragic death, she had been unutterably sad, but she'd never felt such utter desolation and despair as she did now. Grey dawn was fingering the curtains before she fell into a exhausted sleep.

Lyall came to slowly and lay for a while, drifting, before unkind memory jerked her fully awake. A quick apprehensive glance reassured her that she was alone in the bed, and though a fire had been lit there was no sign of Jordan.

Moving like a very old woman, she showered and dressed in a grey wool skirt and cherry-red jumper. She felt oddly calm, almost numb, yet written on her mind in letters of fire was one thought: *she must get away.*

Going to the front window, she looked out. The Jaguar was half buried by drifting snow, but today was one of those perfect winter days that come all too rarely. From a cloudless sky of gentian-blue, sun poured, golden as honey. It gilded the snowy trees, ricocheted from the ice-fringed mere, and turned a row of slowly melting icicles along the eaves to molten gold.

An overwhelming longing seized her to be free, outdoors, to have the cold air and sun on her face. Her hand was on the bolt when she heard the back door open and the sound of feet being stamped on the mat. Her hand fell, and she turned hastily.

Jordan, wearing his sheepskin jacket, his dark curly hair ruffled, was bringing in logs, a scattering of sawdust clinging to his trousers suggested he'd been cutting a fresh supply.

'Lunch ready?' His voice was neutral, neither friendly nor unfriendly.

Lyall glanced at the round battery clock on the kitchen wall and saw it was almost one o'clock. 'Give me a few minutes,' she said.

While a pan of thick, tasty soup heated she made some cheese sandwiches, and carrying bowls, plates, and cutlery through to the lounge put them on the table.

Jordan was tucking in with a healthy appetite when he paused to ask, 'Why aren't you eating?'

'I don't feel like anything.'

He frowned. 'You've hardly eaten a thing since we came.'

'I'm not hungry. I think it's being inside all day.' It was

more than that. Much more. But that would serve as an excuse.

'You must eat something.' Taking the other bowl, he ladled soup into it and placed it in front of her.

She looked at it silently, mutinously.

'Come on,' he coaxed. 'Eat it up like a good girl.'

Emboldened by his manner, she said in a rush, 'Jordan, it's such a lovely day, please can we go out?'

He saw the pleading in her green eyes, noted the hands unconsciously clenched together, and answered quite gently, 'When we've had some lunch, we'll go for a walk. Though we'll have to stick to the lane.'

'Oh, thank you!' She was almost pathetically grateful.

Having passed her a sandwich, he waited pointedly until she picked up her spoon, before continuing with his own lunch. Though his appetite was good, his eating was as neat and fastidious as his other personal habits.

Despite being almost choked by her burning eagerness to get out, Lyall managed to swallow a few spoonfuls of soup and eat one of the sandwiches to satisfy him. As soon as he'd finished, she pulled on her anorak and boots and donned a woolly hat and mitts.

It was thawing fast, but it still felt bitterly cold when they got outside. 'Are you sure you're going to be warm enough?' Jordan asked.

She nodded. 'Quite sure.'

The cottage was built of local slate, and the long, low building, with its overhanging eaves and crooked chimney, had an air of cosy belonging. Perhaps at one time, before being modernised, it had been part of a farm. To the right lay a conglomeration of outbuildings. The one fronting the road served as a garage, the others, storeplaces for fuel and tools.

Leaving the grey-green buildings behind them, they began to walk along the snowy lane. Jordan was bareheaded, his only concession to the weather the turned-up collar of his jacket. It was slow-going and tiring, at times they were almost knee-deep, and Lyall's feet were soon cold and wet in fashion boots intended for city streets. But, dreading having to return to Drum Cottage, she kept doggedly on.

From time to time they talked, by tacit consent keeping the topics light and general. In answer to Jordan's query, Lyall admitted that it was her first visit to the Lakes. He, it transpired, knew them well, having spent quite a number of his boyhood holidays in and around Ambleside.

'We had a holiday cottage,' he told her. 'Mother and Dad enjoyed walking, and we owned a two-handed dinghy we used to sail on Lake Windermere.'

'Your father and yourself?'

'Paul and myself.' Hunching his shoulders, Jordan thrust his hands into his pockets. 'We got on well as boys, though a five-year age-gap meant I was always leader.'

But, even without the age difference, Jordan would have been the leader, the one in charge, Lyall felt sure.

The mention of Paul's name had jolted and depressed her. The sun still shone, but all at once the air had lost its sparkle. She felt colder, constraint hung over them, and the conversation faltered and died.

The winter world was deserted and strangely hushed. The call of a bird was muted, and a hidden stream slipped along with a rustle like silken petticoats. They must be approaching the main road by now, but so far she had heard no sound of passing traffic.

Excitement rising, Lyall came to a decision—or had it been at the back of her mind all the time? If any vehicle came along, she would run into the road and flag it down. All she had to do was beg for help, say she was being held against her will. Not even her husband would be allowed to do that.

Hiding her excitement as best she could, she kept walking. Jordan mustn't guess what she had in mind. The only chance of her plan succeeding was to take him by surprise.

But when they had almost reached the road her heart dropped like a stone; it was snow-covered and obviously impassable.

All at once, through the trees to their right, Lyall saw a man quite close and coming towards them. He was tall and burly, dressed in a khaki-green hunting jacket and cap. He carried a gun under his arm, and a black labrador, tail waving, was ploughing through the snow at his side.

She had stepped forward, her lips parted to call out to him, when she was seized and swung round. 'All right, darling,' Jordan said clearly, 'I apologise.'

Before she could utter a word she was pulled close against him and his mouth was on hers, effectively gagging her. Arms pinned to her sides, feet neatly hooked from beneath her, she was completely off balance and unable to struggle.

She was dimly aware that the man, clearly believing they were lovers making up after a tiff, had altered course and was walking away from them. Jerking her head, she made a frantic effort to free her mouth, but Jordan ruthlessly deepened the kiss until she was half suffocated and her mind was reeling.

His lips had been cold at first, his embrace merely a preventative measure, but after a few moments the quality of his kiss changed, becoming warm and passionate.

Heat ran through her bloodstream and she had to fight against an almost overwhelming desire to put her arms around his neck and return his kiss with an answering passion.

When he finally lifted his head his tawny eyes glinted almost feverishly, a dull flush lay along his high cheekbones, and he breathed as if he'd been running a race. Thickly he said, 'If you ever try anything like that again . . .'

He left the threat unfinished, but she felt herself shiver, and it wasn't with cold.

Grasping her arm, he turned her forcibly back the way they'd come. She could sense that, as well as being angry with her, he was furious with himself for wanting her.

It added a new and frightening aspect to an already fraught relationship. And there was yet another dimension. It was bad enough being an unwilling victim to Jordan's 'lovemaking' but worse to be an unwilling participant. It made her feel humiliated, bitterly angry, that her mind—her will—had so little control over her reactions.

The sun had gone now, leaving a sky of icy pearl. Dusk was stealing out of hiding, and in the dark woods an owl hooted with melancholy mirth . . .

Weary and chilled to the bone, Lyall was more than glad when they reached the cottage. While Jordan kicked the whitish embers of the fire into life and piled on fresh logs, she pulled off her anorak and boots.

Straightening, she found him watching her, and with a jolt saw that he was still aroused. She flinched away from the look of naked desire as if from the heat of a furnace.

He smiled grimly at the involuntary movement, and came towards her purposefully. She wanted to turn and run, but where was there to run to? He took her chin, his thumb stroking along her jaw. Heart racing, Lyall closed her eyes and waited for his kiss with an almost painful intensity.

She gave a little cry and her eyes flew open as he pinched her ear before moving away.

Trembling with reaction, she took a full minute to pull herself together enough to go into the kitchen and start preparing the evening meal.

Over dinner Jordan broke the silence for the first time to ask, 'When did you meet Paul?'

Lyall dropped her fork with a clatter as she jumped at the suddenness of the question. Then as levelly as possible she answered, 'Early in July.'

'Where?'

'Mitch belongs to the firm's Sports and Social Club. I went with her to one of their riverboat discos, and Paul was there.'

'Tell me about it.' It was an order.

Reluctant to talk about Paul, she dipped her head, her lashes dark fans on her pale cheeks. 'There's not much to tell. He came over and spoke to us, then he asked me to dance.'

Paul had made a dead set for her and never left her side all evening. She could see him now in casual black trousers and a white striped shirt, his blond frizzy hair seeming to crackle with electricity, his blue eyes sparkling.

A few years older than herself, but somehow far younger, he was a golden boy as yet wholly unscathed by life's tragedies. He had been good company, extrovert, light hearted and funny, riding high, full of life, his loose-limbed body never still. She hadn't guessed then how moody he could be . . . or how far-reaching the consequences of their meeting . . .

'Then what happened?' Jordan's voice cut through her thoughts, jerking her head up.

'We'd gone by bus because David was away on a course. When Paul found out, he insisted on driving us home.'

'And after that?'

'He just kept on calling,' Lyall replied flatly.

'When did he start giving you presents?'

She flushed scarlet. It had been barely a week after their first meeting. When he had found out that the following day was her birthday, he'd turned up with a diamond-like 'teardrop' on a thin gold chain. It was simple and pretty, and she had accepted it without giving a thought to its possible value.

It was Mitch who had picked it up and gazed at it, her forget-me-not blue eyes popping. 'Wowee! He's either got money to burn, or he's just robbed a jewellers.'

'You don't think it's real, do you?' Lyall had asked uneasily.

'Well, let's put it this way—anyone who dishes out trinkets like that to a girl he's only just met, has either gone overboard in a big way or he's nutty as a fruitcake.'

'Oh, dear. Perhaps I'd better give him it back.' But when she'd made an attempt to return his gift he had been so hurt she hadn't had the heart to persist.

With hindsight she could see that failure to assert herself had set a pattern. Each time Paul had brought or sent her a gift she'd protested, and he had promised, 'No more,' but he'd never kept his word. He had always made light of the cost, saying, 'And I get such a lot of pleasure giving you nice things.'

She became aware that Jordan was watching her through narrowed eyes, and knew she must look harassed and guilty.

'*When*, Lyall?' he pressed.

'On my birthday,' she admitted unhappily.

His firm mouth twisted. 'So from the fifteenth of July onwards Paul spent every cent he could lay his hands on, on you.'

She said nothing. What could she say? It was probably the truth.

Relentlessly, Jordan went on, 'When did he ask you to marry him? He did ask you?'

'Yes . . . Yes, he did. It was early November.'

'And you refused him?'

She nodded mutely.

'By this time I'd realised he was being taken for a ride and cut off his allowance, so most of the presents must have stopped.' Jordan's tone had an edge like a whetted knife.

'It had nothing to do with that,' Lyall denied strenuously. 'I'd known from the start that I couldn't get serious about him, but for a time he kept things light and I didn't realise how involved he was getting.'

'And even when you did, you kept on taking his gifts.'

It was an indictment she couldn't deny. Although she was strong in many ways, Lyall had lacked the ruthlessness necessary to wound him. Paul, she could see now, had taken advantage of that fact. He had used her weakness to try to gain his own ends, hoping to coerce her into marrying him in the same way he'd coerced her into accepting his gifts.

The evening he'd proposed to her had been a traumatic one. Mitch had gone out and they were alone in the flat. Paul's moods had been getting steadily worse during the preceding weeks, often swinging between black despair and spirits so high that they held an edge of hysteria.

'He's next door to loopy,' Mitch had said on more than one occasion. 'Take my advice and give him his marching orders.'

But Lyall had been caught, unable to free herself from the emotional web her concern and affection for him had spun. Despite her reluctance to hurt him, however, she knew there was no way she could marry him.

He'd cajoled and pleaded and finally, on his knees, wept. Her soft heart going out to him, she had put her arms around his shaking shoulders.

'We could make a go of it, I know we could,' he had insisted.

'It wouldn't work, really it wouldn't. I don't love you,' she had repeated for the umpteenth time.

'But you don't find me repulsive?' He had sounded like a child begging for reassurance.

'Of course I don't find you repulsive. You know I don't. I think you're a most attractive man and I like you very much, but it takes more than that to make a marriage work. I'll need to love the man I marry.'

'I could make you love me, I know I could,' he had muttered.

'No one can make another person love them. Love is something either you feel or you don't. It isn't something you can order.'

'All right,' he had cried, 'marry me without loving me. God knows, I love you enough for two. I'm mad about you,

Lyall. I don't know what I'll do if you don't marry me.'

'I'll tell you what you'll do . . .' She had made an effort to sound bracing. 'You'll put me right out of your mind and find yourself a woman who can love you the way a wife should.'

'There's no other woman I want. There's not another girl in the world who can compare with you.'

'Nonsense,' she had said briskly. 'The world is full of girls who could leave me standing.'

He shook his head, dismissing her words. 'I'm crazy about you. I can't sleep for wanting you.'

'And I'm very fond of you. You must see the two just don't match up.' She had taken his face between her hands. It had looked white and pinched with misery. 'I'm sorry, truly I am,' she had said gently, 'but there's no way I can marry you. Come on now.' She had tried to laugh to ease the tension. 'Let's have you up before you get housemaid's knee!'

Apparently realising that he couldn't budge her, Paul had seized her hands, holding them in a grip that hurt. 'You won't stop seeing me? Promise you won't stop seeing me?'

She had hesitated. She *should* stop seeing him, make a clean break, for his sake . . .

'If you won't see me again, I might as well kill myself!' he had cried wildly.

Shocked, she had ordered, 'Don't say such a terrible thing!'

'I mean it.' There had been no mistaking his desperation. 'If you stop seeing me, there'll be nothing left to live for . . .'

Jordan leaned forward to pour more wine into Lyall's glass. 'So tell me what happened when Paul proposed.'

She looked up, her beautiful green eyes shadowed. 'I . . . I'd rather not talk about it.'

'I'm sure you would,' he agreed grimly. 'But I want to know. And don't give me a whitewashed version; I want the truth.'

So she told him, her voice low, scarcely above a whisper at times, and he watched her steadily, his eyes amber and unblinking as a cat's.

She spoke the bare truth, making no explanations or excuses, ending, 'He wanted me to promise to go on seeing him. He said if I didn't there was nothing left to live for and he might as well kill himself.'

'Did you promise?' Jordan demanded sharply.

'Yes. In the mood he was in, I was afraid not to.' She brushed a hand over her eyes. 'I thought it would be easier to break it off gradually. I can see now it was the wrong thing to do. He just clung tighter, hoping he could change my mind.'

'And, getting even more desperate when he couldn't, he started to hit the bottle.' Jordan's voice was hard and accusing.

She nodded miserably. Paul's reckless bouts of drinking had terrified her. 'I wish to God I hadn't promised. I wish I'd called his bluff.'

'Do you think it *was* bluff?' Jordan sat up and questioned with an edge to his tone.

'That's just it,' she said. 'Mitch believed it was, but I couldn't be sure. I only wish I had stopped seeing him then, before it was too late.'

'It was already too late,' Jordan said bleakly. 'By that time he probably considered he'd bought you.'

Her throat tightened at the unkind words, and she

swallowed hard. With a touch of desperation she asked, 'So what should I have done? Married him without loving him? Even if I could have brought myself to do it, how long do you think a marriage like that would have lasted?'

'As long as the presents kept flowing,' Jordan answered cynically.

'I never wanted his presents in the first place.' Lyall pressed distracted fingers to her temples.

'But when you refused to marry him, you didn't give him them back.'

'I tried,' she said wearily. 'But he wouldn't take them.'

'You could have *sent* them to him. Don't tell me why you didn't,' he added caustically. 'I can guess. You didn't want to hurt him.'

'No, I didn't!' she cried, at the end of her tether. 'I know you'll never believe that, but it's the truth. If I hadn't cared about hurting him I wouldn't have let things go on for so long. If I hadn't cared about hurting him it would have been easy to end it. Dear God, don't you think I blame myself? I would have loved him if I could.' It was a cry from the heart.

For a moment Jordan looked shaken, but only for a moment. His lip curling, he said, 'I feel I should applaud. Tell me, where do you get such acting talent from?'

Her hands clenched as a hot tide of anger and resentment engulfed her. Biting her lower lip, she fought for control. When she had achieved an outward semblance of it, she rose and said in a voice devoid of feeling, 'I'll get the fruit and coffee.'

The meal finally over, she cleared the table and washed the dishes, stacking them neatly away. With nothing left to do, she still lingered, loath to join Jordan. She was so tired, drained and exhausted. If only she could go to bed.

No, she thought violently, *not bed.* Yet she could hardly spend the remainder of the evening skulking in the kitchen.

An old Neil Diamond tape was playing softly. Jordan had a wide taste in music, she had discovered, a taste that coincided well with her own. It ranged from the best of pop through to classical music and grand opera.

She had been a trifle surprised to find that, on the whole, he preferred the romantic composers. Yet, on reflection, didn't that fit in with his love of poetry? And, though usually very self-controlled, he was a man of deep feelings, strong passions. If he loved a woman it would be wholly, completely, no half measures. The same way he would hate.

She shivered.

Her legs stiff and reluctant, she forced herself to go through to the lounge, which was dimly lit. He was sitting by the fire, the flickering flames turning his lean face into a bronze mask. In his hands he held the little snowstorm she'd bought him with so much love, such happy anticipation.

She sat on the couch, as far away from him as possible, but her eyes were drawn to the long fingers curved around the glass, as if merely touching it gave him pleasure. All at once she was overwhelmed by pain so intense that she had to catch her underlip in her teeth to prevent a moan escaping.

He glanced up and she looked hurriedly away, but not before he had glimpsed the misery and desolation she had been unable to hide.

'You look shattered,' he said shortly. 'Why don't you go to bed?'

Without a word, she got to her feet and headed blindly for the bathroom.

After dark the wind had changed, bringing cloud and warmer air from the west. For a long time Lyall lay in the big bed, tense and apprehensive, listening to the drip, drip of melting snow and ice. When Jordan showed no sign of joining her she gradually relaxed and, from one moment to the next, slipped over the brink of consciousness into sleep.

It was a troubled sleep that some time during the night spawned bad dreams. She was stumbling along a dark underground passage with some nameless horror at her heels, when suddenly the tunnel ended in a wall of solid rock. She was trapped, while the thing that stalked her came closer and closer.

Any second it would reach out of the darkness and touch her . . .

She gave a terrified scream and began to struggle convulsively.

'Gently now, gently,' a voice soothed. Her head was cradled against a muscular shoulder, while a hand stroked her hair. 'It's all right . . . Everything's all right.'

Gradually the raw-edged panic subsided, her breathing slowed, and the heavy thudding of her heart eased. With a feeling of being safe and cared for, she nestled against the man who was holding her, her damp cheek pressed against the warm, smooth skin of his chest.

CHAPTER SIX

LYALL awoke with a strange feeling of well-being, and for a while lay savouring it, before her mind emerged fully from the mists of sleep. She was alone, but clearly Jordan had slept beside her.

A hazy memory tugged at her mind. She'd had a nightmare and he'd held her close, consoled her . . . But that was most unlikely. It was more probable that the whole thing had been a dream, born of her longing for some kindness and comfort.

The curtains had been drawn back, and as she got out of bed Lyall could see a weak sun trying to struggle through a rent in the clouds. The snow was still thawing fast. Beyond the mere a boisterous wind played tag with the bare branches of the trees, and pounced on the sparse bushes huddled nervously by the reed-fringed water. As she watched, a small flock of birds rose from the pines and were tossed like pieces of litter into the windy sky.

She had just finished dressing when the sound of a car engine starting, then stopping, made her hurry to the window. Her breath misted on the pane and she wiped it clear with her fingers to peer through.

Jordan was just getting out of the Jaguar. He'd moved melting snow from around the car, and as she watched he picked up a spade and with strong, rhythmic movements began to clear a way to the garage.

A cardboard carton on the breakfast bar caught Lyall's

eye. It contained a loaf of brown bread, two cartons of milk and a paper, obviously delivered that morning.

The roads must be clear. Excitement made her mouth go dry. Perhaps she could get away today, get back to London while the flat was still available. In the rush of wedding preparations she had forgotten to cancel the lease. Now that would prove a blessing. If she could get her grandfather moved in there, her biggest worry would be over. But she must do it before he could be installed in the penthouse. Once she allowed that to happen, Jordan's hold on her would be immeasurably strengthened. With her grandfather's precarious state of health she dared not risk too much of an upheaval.

The thing that worried her most was how to break it to Joe that she had left Jordan. While telling him plainly that she'd had no alternative, she would have to make as light of the situation as possible to try and spare him too much worry. Though it was bound to come as a shock to him.

Once that hurdle was safely over, the next would be money. The fact that the rent on the flat had been paid in advance was a boon, but even so she'd have to find some work quickly.

Mitch would help in any way she could, Lyall knew, and felt immensely cheered. She could tell the blonde girl the whole sorry story and be sure of her support, both moral and practical . . .

Lyall was still deep in thought when she realised Jordan had come in and seemed to be busy in the kitchen. She could smell toast and hear the clatter of crockery.

'Thought *I'd* get lunch today for a change,' he said, appearing with a tray holding a bowl of salad and a plate of toasted sandwiches, some of which were distinctly charred around the edges. 'Though I'm afraid I never did get my black belt for cooking,' he added gravely. Then, gently tugging a tendril of her dark silky hair, he mused, 'Still, a curl or two might suit you.'

She looked at him blankly.

His gold-flecked eyes dancing, he asked, 'Did your grandmother never tell you the one about burnt toast making your hair curl?'

'Oh, yes.' She found herself smiling back, her spirits lifting because he was in such a good mood. 'But I'm afraid I didn't believe her.'

He shook his head reprovingly. 'O ye of little faith. After a couple of those you'll look like Topsy.'

'Perhaps I'd better stick to one then,' she said in mock alarm. 'I don't want to overdo it.'

'Coward,' he taunted, grinning.

Her heart seemed to turn right over; today he was more like the man she'd fallen in love with.

Jordan ate a couple of the sandwiches before admitting, 'Maybe discretion is the better part of valour. If I go on like this my stomach will never forgive me.'

She laughed at his droll expression.

His eyes on her lovely face, he said abruptly, 'You should laugh more often, it suits you.' In his glance was a lick of flame, a sexual awareness that made her body burn with heat.

It would take only a movement, a look, on her part . . . Silently she fought for control over the treacherous urge, and won. Jerkily she said, 'I haven't had much to laugh about lately.'

His lips tightened and, regretting her words, she asked

the first thing that came into her head. 'Have you put the car away?'

'No. I thought I'd take you out.'

'Out?' She could scarcely believe he meant it.

'The roads should be clear enough for a drive this afternoon. Would you like that?'

'Oh, yes.' She made no attempt to hide her eagerness, her desire to escape these four walls.

After they had fruit and coffee, Jordan pulled a jacket over his Arran sweater and went out again.

Lyall heard the car engine start and, after running for a short while, stop. As soon as she'd cleared away the remnants of the meal she went to the front window and looked out. The bonnet of the car was up and Jordan was tinkering in the engine.

How alike men were, she thought with wry humour. She had often seen Paul do the same. He had taught her to drive his black Escort, but quite frequently half her 'lesson' had been lost while he poked about under the bonnet.

Despite this she had passed her test first time and he had boasted, 'Well, what else did you expect, with an expert teacher like me? And you wanted to go to a driving school . . .'

The slam of the car's bonnet being dropped into place brought her head up. A few seconds later the back door opened and Jordan came in, wiping his hands on a piece of cotton waste. Shrugging out of his jacket, he vanished into the bathroom, saying cheerfully, 'Won't be long.'

As she thought of the car standing ready outside, Lyall's heart began to beat in a rapid tattoo. Jordan's hands had been oily when he came in, he'd been wiping them . . . He must have left the keys in the ignition.

Excitement almost choking her, she edged towards the front door. The bolt had been drawn back; all she had to do was open it quietly and slip out . . .

She was outside, the door closed behind her, before she considered that she had neither coat nor handbag. But there should be enough petrol in the Jaguar's tank to get her quite a few miles, then she would think of something.

Her legs curiously stiff and alien, her heart banging against her ribs, Lyall hurried to the car and climbed in. She'd never driven anything so big and powerful before, but she'd soon get the hang of it. Reaching to turn the key, she found the ignition was empty.

The shock of disappointment hit her like a fist in the solar plexus. Pulling herself together, she closed the car door as quietly as possible and, knowing how useless it would be, fought down the temptation to take to her heels and run.

A Yale lock meant the front door couldn't be opened from the outside without a key. Panic, in case Jordan had already missed her, made her feel sick as she crept through the small wooden gate between the house and garage, and slipped in the back way.

To her untold relief he was still in the bathroom and, judging by the running water, taking a shower.

It was a moment or two before she caught sight of the jacket he'd slung across the back of one of the dining chairs. Fool! she berated herself silently. That's where the keys would be.

The shower was still running. Palms damp with perspiration, Lyall began to search through his jacket with frantic haste. As she turned it, his wallet slipped from one of the inside pockets and fell to the floor, opening to show a snap of Jordan and a blonde woman. Snatching it up, she closed it and thrust it back, then felt in the one remaining pocket.

As she did so some sixth sense made her glance up. Jordan was standing in the doorway, a towel knotted around his lean hips, watching her.

'Looking for something?' he asked softly.

Caught like a criminal, her hand still in his jacket pocket, she stared at him while a tide of scalding colour flooded into her face.

'These perhaps?' He held up the keys, dangling them mockingly between a finger and thumb.

She made a little choked sound and jerked her hand free. Slowly the colour drained from her face, leaving her paper-white.

'Do you take me for a complete fool?' he asked trenchantly.

Sinking into the nearest chair, she covered her face with trembling hands. It was almost as if he'd expected her to try and get away, engineered the whole charade. Had it been a kind of torture by hope? If it had, then he was good at it, she conceded bitterly. His apparent softening might have been designed just to give her a false sense of security. As it had.

Jordan had vanished from view, but the bathroom door was a little ajar, letting a rectangle of light spill across the polished floor of the bedroom. All at once Lyall began to shiver and, needing the warmth and comfort it offered, she went to huddle by the fire.

Her thoughts went to the photograph in his wallet. Though she'd seen it for only a split second it was engraved on her mind. It had been a holiday snapshot of him and a beautiful fair-haired woman standing by a log cabin. His arm had been around her shoulders and she'd been smiling up at him. There'd been something about the pose that had suggested the intimacy of lovers rather than the companionship of friends.

Lyall had always accepted that there must have been plenty of women in his past, but she'd told herself firmly that what had happened before he met her didn't matter. Now, as he hated her, and it wasn't a proper marriage, perhaps it mattered even less. Yet that smiling face stayed in her mind, sharp as a piece of jagged glass in a wound.

Needing an escape from her painful thoughts, Lyall reached into the alcove for a book, taking the first one that came to hand. Though it was still early afternoon, the sky had darkened and the day was so gloomy that she had to switch on the standard lamp to see. Opening the book, she began to read: 'Last night I dreamt I went to Manderley again . . .'

Rebecca was one of her favourite books, and she was engrossed when, without a flicker of warning, the light went out. Wondering if the bulb had gone, she tried the main light. That failed to come on; so did the kitchen one.

She was just digesting this when Jordan appeared wearing well cut brown trousers with an off-white sweater, and asked, 'All the lights gone?'

'I think so.'

He grunted. 'Probably the main fuse has blown. I'd better fix it before we go.'

So he was still taking her. Her spirits lifted somewhat.

'There's a card of fuse wire on top of the cupboard,' she volunteered, having noticed it there when she'd taken some tinned stuff from the shelves.

He nodded and went into the storeroom, the white door creaking very slightly as it swung to after him.

Lyall realised two things simultaneously. He'd put the car keys down on the breakfast bar, and there were bolts top and bottom on the outside of the storeroom door.

She acted instinctively, without stopping to think. Slamming the door shut, she pushed home the bolts and made a grab for the keys. Her frantic lunge sent them skittering off the bar and under the edge of the sink unit, and she lost precious seconds while she scrabbled for them. Her fingers had just closed around the cold metal when the first blow shuddered against the door panels. How long would the frail bolts hold?

Running for the front door, she pulled it open and, clutching the keys so tightly they cut into her hand, fled down the steps. Her foot slipped off the bottom one and she went sprawling, all the breath knocked out of her.

Somehow she picked herself up and struggled into the car, pulling the door closed. Her hands were shaking so much that it took three attempts to fit the right key into the ignition and turn it.

Immediately the powerful engine purred into life. As she engaged first gear and the car started to move forward, the door was suddenly wrenched open. A steely hand clamped around her wrist while the other reached to turn off the ignition and remove the keys.

She gave a little cry as Jordan hauled her out unceremoniously. Lyall lost her cool, and began to struggle wildly.

'You little hellcat!' he snarled, as one of her small fists caught him in the face. 'Will you be still?' Holding her clamped to him with one arm, he slammed the car door and locked it, before hustling her back into the cottage and through to the kitchen.

Lyall gasped aloud at the sight of the storeroom door. It was hanging drunkenly from its hinges, one panel split from top to bottom, both bolts torn away from the splintered wood. A hand to her mouth, she stared at it with huge, scared eyes.

'Yes,' he said grimly. 'A mess, isn't it? I doubt very much if "honeymoon games" will sound a reasonable explanation.'

He steered her ahead of him into the storeroom, and she stood by helplessly while he crouched to check the fuses and replace the one which had blown. When he'd finished, he tried the kitchen light and gave a murmur of satisfaction as it came on. Then he turned to her, his glance raking her from head to foot.

Knowing that this time she must have angered him beyond endurance, and half expecting physical violence, she had to make an effort not to cringe away. But he made no move to touch her, merely ordering curtly, 'You'd better go and get yourself tidied up.'

Reprieved, at least for the time being, Lyall hurried into the bathroom. A look in one of the long mirrors showed a sorry sight. Her hair was dishevelled, her clothes awry.

Having combed her hair and tucked her fine wool blouse neatly back into her skirt, she took her courage in a death grip and, trying not to think of the retribution almost certainly awaiting her, returned to the living-room.

Jordan was sitting by the fire staring into the flames, his

face half averted. Lyall stood silently, waiting for his wrath to descend on her. But he studiously ignored her, and after hesitating for some moments she sank into the opposite chair.

Tension stretched like invisible wires between them until she thought she would scream. Hands clenched, she fought to keep a grip on her nerves. Why didn't he speak?

Then, suddenly deciding she wouldn't meekly play it his way, she burst out, 'If you're waiting for me to say I'm sorry about the damage to the door—well, I won't!'

He looked across at her, a dangerous gleam in his amber eyes. 'That's not the only thing you won't do. My patience is at an end. I don't want any repeat of this afternoon's escapade. Understood?' There was a note of quiet menace in his soft voice which chilled her.

If he'd stormed and shouted, she felt she could have faced it better than this deadly calm, this kid-glove method of bringing her to heel.

When she failed to answer, he went on, 'I want your promise that you won't try anything like that again.'

She stared down at the hands clasped tightly together in her lap.

'Well?'

Lyall shook her head mutely. It was a promise she wasn't prepared to give.

'Do you expect me to tolerate your tricks?'

She jumped to her feet, her breasts heaving. 'Do you expect me to stay here and be crucified for something I didn't do?'

Jordan rose in one swift movement and his hands shot out and fastened around the soft flesh of her upper arms. 'What did you hope to achieve by running away? I wouldn't have let you go. You're my wife and you'll stay my wife until I'm ready to get rid of you.'

'If I'd managed to get to London . . .' she began defiantly, then broke off.

His grip tightened. 'What did you intend to do if you'd managed to get to London?'

She squirmed and made a futile effort to pull his hands away. 'You're hurting me!'

'Then suppose you answer my question.'

'I wanted to see Grandad, to tell him at least part of the truth.'

'Didn't you think that might be a risk?'

'Yes,' she said almost in a whisper. 'But it was a risk I felt I had to take.'

'Why, Lyall?' His fingers tightened even more.

Knowing he wouldn't let her go until he was satisfifed, she admitted huskily, 'I wanted to get him moved into the flat I'd rented. I . . . I didn't cancel the lease . . .'

At last his grip slackened, as if he'd learnt what he wanted to know. What he'd already suspected. Casually he said, 'No, but I did.'

'What?' she breathed.

'I cancelled the lease on the flat.' He said it as if talking to a not very bright child.

'It was nothing to do with you,' she choked. 'You had no right to do any such thing!'

'I had every right. You're my wife and you're going to live with me.'

'I won't!' There, she'd said it. 'I won't live with you. There's no way you can make me.'

'Don't you think so?' He sounded quite cool and unperturbed. 'What about your grandfather?'

'We'll manage somehow. I won't let him be moved into your apartment.'

'My dear Lyall, you can't prevent it.'

'I *can* prevent it!' Her voice had risen.

'If necessary, I'll tell him the whole truth. The real reason you married me.'

'I don't think so. When you're not so upset and overwrought your common sense will show you that it's far too much of a gamble. Surely you don't want *his* death on your conscience as well?'

Her face went so white, Jordan thought for a moment she was going to faint.

'In any case,' he went on flatly, 'it's too late.'

'Too late? What do you mean, too late?' she demanded fearfully.

'Your grandfather is already living in my apartment. As soon as you agreed to marry me I went ahead and had some rooms converted for his use. The firm I employed sent men in immediately, and the work was completed even before our wedding. I arranged, with Joe's co-operation, of course, to have him taken straight to my place after the ceremony, instead of back to the home.'

'I don't believe you,' she protested faintly. 'He would have told me.'

'We agreed to keep it a secret. He didn't want you to spoil your honeymoon by fretting about getting back to him.'

Yes, that sounded like Joe, Lyall thought.

Jordan released his hold and she sank limply down into the chair. Her arms crossed over her chest, her hands holding her upper arms, she rocked herself backwards and forwards, agitation making her unable to sit still as she took in what he had told her.

After a moment she cried almost pleadingly, 'But I don't understand. How will he manage? Who . . . who is there to look after him? He needs special care.'

'Oh, he'll be fine. He has Duggan.'

'Duggan? Who's Duggan?'

'Patrick Duggan is a cheerful, intelligent, fully qualified nurse. The ideal man for the job. He'll take good care of Joe and make him an excellent companion.'

Suddenly seeing exactly what Jordan intended, she cried, 'Gaoler, don't you mean?'

'Certainly not,' he denied crisply. 'Your grandfather won't be a prisoner, merely a . . . hostage for your good behaviour. Things won't be so bad if you're sensible.'

'Damn you!' she muttered. 'You had all this planned from the start. Didn't you?' Her temper rose. '*Didn't you?*'

'Yes, this was the way I planned it,' he admitted calmly. 'I couldn't let you just walk out of the door the first time I turned my back.'

'You're a fiend,' she said bitterly. 'How could you use a sick old man like that? Oh, I can't bear Grandad being a virtual prisoner because of what you think I did. I can't bear it!'

Jordan took her face in both hands and lifted it. 'Stop being foolish,' he told her quite gently. 'I've just told you he won't be anything of the kind. He'll have far more freedom with Duggan to take him out and about than he'd have had cooped up in a tiny flat all day while you were out working.'

His fingers brushed her cheek lightly. The action had something of tenderness in it, but as she stared up at him, his face tightened as if he was annoyed with himself for allowing her distress to get under his guard.

Briskly he went on, 'And Duggan's no gaoler. I'll be greatly surprised if your grandfather hasn't taken to him, and the pair aren't getting on like a house on fire. He's a nice bloke, calm and down-to-earth, with a strong sense of humour. He's also a very good chess player. He looked after my father during his last illness; that's how I got to know him so well. We're really lucky to get him.

'He's been nursing a retired MP for the past couple of years and would still be with him if the honourable gentleman hadn't decided to go to the Isle of Man to live with his widowed sister. Despite his name, Duggan is a Cockney born and bred, and no inducement would get him to leave London. That's our good fortune.'

Lyall felt a little glow of warmth. In spite of his anger, he was going out of his way to try to reassure her.

'Joe won't have a single cause to worry,' Jordan went on, 'unless you give him one. If you do, then any setback to his health will be on your own conscience. If you love him as much as you claim to, however, all you need to do to make everything in the garden lovely is convince him you're really happy. If you're as good an actress as I believe you are, that shouldn't prove to be too difficult.'

His words were like a slap in the face after his previous kindness.

Stung, she jumped to her feet and cried hoarsely, 'I hate you!'

'Temper . . .' he chided.

Biting her lip, she turned sharply away and, needing to do something to help dissipate the dizzying rush of adrenalin, took a shower, changed into a moss-green dress, and went through to the kitchen to start preparing the evening meal.

So he'd won, she conceded bitterly. For her grandfather's sake she was going to have to play the role Jordan had cast her in. The role of a happy wife.

If theirs had been a normal marriage, if only Jordan had loved her and not held her responsible for Paul's death, it would have been so easy. As it was, it would be the hardest thing she'd ever had to do in her life.

How long could she endure it? she wondered. Was there any hope that Jordan would ever believe her? And if a miracle happened and he did, what then? Probably he'd let her have a quiet divorce. The thought gave her no pleasure. Though it was the best she could hope for, she told herself bleakly.

The meal, a silent one, was over and they were having coffee on the settee in front of the fire before Jordan looked up to ask abruptly, 'You say the jewellery Paul gave you wasn't very valuable, just costume stuff?'

Shock ran along her nerve-ends, and almost in a whisper she answered, 'Most of it was.'

'How much did you get for it?'

She told him, and watched the disbelief on his face. If she hadn't had to sell Paul's gifts she could have *shown* Jordan they weren't the gold and precious stones he believed them to be. Now there seemed no way she could prove it.

'I don't suppose you got an itemised bill of sale?' he asked sardonically.

If only she had. 'If only' must be the two saddest, most futile words in the English language. But the man behind the counter, after chatting idly while he examined the pieces, had simply offered her a lump sum. It had seemed a fair amount and, more important, had covered what she needed so desperately.

Feeling distressed and guilty at having to sell the things Paul had given her, all she had wanted to do was get the transaction over and escape from the shop. Having accepted the jeweller's offer, she had been paid in cash and that had been that. She had put the money in her bag and hurried straight round to the estate agent's to pay the advance rent on the flat.

'Well, Lyall?' Jordan pressed.

She shook her head wordlessly.

'Did you always go to the same place?' he asked.

She looked at him blankly.

'To sell your boyfriend's gifts,' he clarified.

'You sound as if you think I'm completely heartless and mercenary! Worse than a kept woman . . .'

'You are worse. A kept woman usually gives value for money. What did you ever give, apart from kisses and worthless promises?' His golden eyes brilliant with contempt, he added, 'You sold yourself, then never came across.'

'That's not true. It's not!' She felt a fierce, primitive desire to hit out at him, to scream and throw things, to rail against fate.

She did nothing of the kind. When she'd manage to regain her self-control, she looked up and said quietly, 'You're quite wrong about me. If you could only forget this blind prejudice you'd see clearly that . . .'

'I can see clearly now,' he broke in. 'I have a *very* clear picture in my mind of Paul being burnt alive.'

'You're a brute,' she muttered hoarsely, hating him for

his cruelty, for what he was putting her through. 'An absolute swine!'

He gave a mirthless laugh and remarked, 'If the American press have got wind of our marriage, I expect Nancy will be saying very much the same.'

'Nancy?' In spite of her anger and agitation Lyall's interest was caught. 'The blonde in the snapshot?' Instantly she wished the words unspoken, but Jordan was looking at her, one dark brow raised. She flushed hotly. 'I saw a photograph in your wallet when I . . . when I . . .'

'When you were rifling my pockets,' he finished trenchantly. 'Yes, that was Nancy. Though I never made her any promises, she was expecting me to go back to the States and marry her.'

'I wish to God you had,' Lyall muttered fervently. 'Or that you'd never left.'

'Now there we differ. I wish to God I'd never gone.' Almost to himself he added, 'I didn't even get the news of Paul's death until two weeks after it happened.'

'So that's why you didn't come to the funeral?'

'That's why. Do you mean to say *you* went?' There was an odd note in his voice.

'Yes . . . Mitch and I.'

'Then you can tell me about it.'

In a strangled whisper she asked, 'Do you really want to know, or is this just another form of torture?'

'I want to know.' He sounded curiously weary.

'There's not much to tell.'

Paul's funeral had taken place on a damp and raw Thursday morning in late November. The small crematorium had been a bleak and melancholy place, with brown leaves scattered underfoot and lying in wet drifts beneath the naked trees. The short service in the bare chapel, with a mere handful of friends as mourners, had been hard to bear. Lyall had stumbled out, her eyes red and swollen, her grief bitter at such a tragic waste of a young life. The sharp, tangy smell of chrysanthemums brought it back vividly. 'Why did you go?' asked Jordan when she had finished speaking. 'Conscience?'

Lyall refused to answer, but her shining oval nails bit deeply, painfully, into her soft palms, while the knuckles of her slender hands turned bone-white.

Watching her closely, Jordan muttered something, and taking both her hands turned the palms uppermost and stared at the purple crescents left by her nails. Then, with a sound almost like a groan, he lifted each palm to his lips. In his dark face there was remorse, and once again that fleeting tenderness.

Pulling her to him, he used one hand to cradle her silky head against his chest, while the other moved up and down her spine in a curiously soothing gesture.

'Jordan,' she said in a choked whisper. 'Oh, Jordan, please believe I'm not the kind of woman you think I am. I never meant to hurt Paul . . .'

He stiffened and, without answering, he dropped his arms away and let her go. For a moment he eyed her wan face, then flatly he said, 'You look all in. You'd better get some sleep.'

Heavily, Lyall went to prepare for bed. She could tell him she'd never meant to hurt Paul until the cows came home, but there was no way she could make him believe it.

When she emerged from the bathroom he was sitting where she'd left him, staring into space. She took a few tentative steps towards him. There was something she wanted to ask, to beg. 'Jordan ...' She hesitated, then plucked up courage. 'How much longer do you intend to stay here?'

He looked at her and raised a dark brow. 'Tired of your honeymoon so soon?'

Ignoring the hated mockery, she said quietly, 'I would like to get back to Grandad.'

Jordan merely looked at her, his eyes cool and speculative. She turned away. It had been foolish of her to ask. Knowing how much she wanted to leave, he would be most unlikely to agree.

Spent and defeated, she went over to the bed and crawled beneath the duvet. She was asleep almost before her head touched the pillow.

CHAPTER SEVEN

JORDAN woke her before it was light with a finger tapping her cheek, not ungently. He was sitting on the edge of the bed, gazing down at her, a curious expression in his tawny eyes. He was shaved and dressed, his peat-coloured hair curling a little, still damp from the shower.

She lay blinking owlishly at him, her eyelids feeling as if they'd been glued together, her head muzzy.

'Had enough sleep?' he asked.

Far from ready to face the day, she mumbled that she was still tired.

'Pity,' he said casually. 'I thought you might like to make an early start back to town.'

Lyall struggled up, pushing back the tumbled dark hair. 'You mean we're going home today?' she asked unbelievingly.

'I thought you wanted to.'

'Oh, I do . . .' She didn't care that he was teasing her. It was enough that they were going back. She made a move to get out of bed.

'There's not that much of a hurry,' he protested. 'You can drink your tea first.'

She drank the tea he'd placed on the cabinet while he lifted their cases from the top of the wardrobe. As soon as the cup was empty she hurried into the bathroom.

By the time she was washed and dressed, Jordan had almost completed his packing, as if now he'd made up his mind to go he could hardly wait to get away. Which suited her just fine.

He refused breakfast, and as soon as she'd finished putting her clothes in her case he fastened it, got the Jaguar out, and put their luggage in the boot.

By nine-thirty everything was tidy and they were ready to leave. He settled her in the car and they drove away from Drum Cottage without a backward glance, as if both were glad to leave it behind them.

When they reached the grey straggle of cottages bordering the road on the outskirts of Brentmere, Jordan stopped the car. As though underlining the hold he had on her, he left the keys in the ignition while he went to number sixteen. This, Lyall, deduced, determinedly ignoring the taunting keys, must be where Mrs Smith lived.

The door was opened promptly to his knock and after a word or two he vanished inside, ducking his head under the low lintel. As well as leaving the keys to the cottage he would need to make arrangements to have the storeroom door repaired. He could hardly tell the truth about what had happened, so what explanation would he give? With a bit of luck, he'd sweat over it.

But when he reappeared he looked so completely unruffled that she knew she'd been foolish to imagine him sweating over anything.

Mrs Smith, a small, sprightly-looking woman with hair the colour and texture of steel wool and an enveloping blue and white sprigged pinafore, followed him to the door. She stood by the step and, her head tilted a shade to one side, her eyes bird-bright with curiosity, peered into the car.

If Jordan had given 'honeymoon games' as the explanation for the broken door, she was probably wondering what kind of Amazon he'd married, Lyall thought wryly, as he got back into the car and lifted a hand in salute before driving off.

Apart from a mantling on the high hills, the snow was almost gone. The road was shiny, crocodile rough, and running with little streams of water. A pewter sky and no breath of wind made the day as grey and placid as a meeting of Quakers.

On the M6 they stopped for petrol and coffee, then later for an early lunch. Impatience to see her grandfather made the journey seem slow, and Lyall was glad when they finally reached Montana House.

As they were wafted smoothly up to the penthouse, Lyall suddenly recalled, with a hollow feeling in the pit of her stomach, the first time Jordan had taken her up in this lift.

He gave her a glinting look and, reading her thoughts with an accuracy which shook her, said trenchantly, 'You came very willingly. But of course you must have been on the look-out for another well-heeled sucker.'

Her teeth clenched, and her face felt stiff with the effort of hiding the misery she refused to let him see.

When they stepped out of the lift, Wilkes's tall, thin figure, with its slight stoop and rounded shoulders, appeared instantly. He met them with a word of welcome and a polite enquiry as to what kind of journey they'd had.

'Excellent, thanks,' answered Jordan. And, handing him the car keys, added, 'Our luggage is still in the boot, when you've got a minute.'

Wilkes inclined his balding head before asking, 'Does Madam wish to look over tonight's menu, in case there are any changes she would care to make?'

Lyall had herself in hand again and answered pleasantly, 'No, thank you, Wilkes. I'm sure that whatever you've chosen will be fine.'

The man looked gratified and not a little relieved, and Lyall realised her advent must have loomed as a threat. With a smile she went on, 'But now there are three extra people and so much more to do, I'll be happy to lend a hand if you need one.'

His pale grey-blue eyes a trifle shocked, he replied, 'Thank you, Madam, but I'm sure that won't be necessary.' Then, suddenly much more human, he admitted, 'Up until now I have been . . . er . . . somewhat under-employed.' With a little bow, he moved away on silent feet.

Eager to see Joe, Lyall would have hurried ahead, but Jordan put a restraining hand on her arm. She hesitated, then advanced at his pace. Quietly he opened the living-room door and they stood looking across the large, attractive room at the two men sitting by the sliding glass panels which gave access to the terrace and garden.

Joe was ensconced in a wheelchair, his back to them, and sitting opposite across the small, round table was a burly young man with thick, carroty hair and a pleasant, good-humoured face. They were playing draughts, a light-hearted game, it was immediately apparent, accompanied by a good deal of badinage.

Lyall was about to speak when a thought made her hesitate. She glanced up at Jordan. He bent his head in response and she whispered in his ear, 'You don't think seeing us unexpectedly will be a shock to him?'

Jordan smiled slightly, then, his lips brushing her ear, whispered back, 'It won't be unexpected. While I was with Mrs Smith I phoned home to let Wilkes know we were on our way. He'll have passed on the good news.'

He thought of everything.

Suddenly he stopped and swept her up. She gave a squeal

of surprise and flung her arms around his neck as he made a pretence of dropping her. Both men looked towards the door. Grinning, Jordan carried her in.

'What are you doing?' protested Lyall.

'Carrying my bride over the threshold,' Jordan answered. 'What else?'

'It's nice to see old traditions being kept up,' remarked Joe, smiling broadly.

'And this is a very old one,' murmured Jordan. 'Carrying a woman over the threshold harks back to the Sabine women. They were reluctant "brides" to say the least.' Dropping a light kiss on Lyall's lips, he set her on her feet.

She gave him a quick, fulminating glance, which he returned with a mocking smile. So this was how he intended to play it! Turning her back on him, she went to her grandfather and bent to kiss his cheek.

'So what are you doing home already?' he scolded.

Home, Lyall noted with a pang. Joe had said the word so naturally, as if he already thought of this luxurious penthouse as home.

'As soon as she knew you were here she couldn't wait to get back,' observed Jordan with perfect truth.

'Didn't you tell her I'd got Duggan?' Joe demanded.

'I told her,' said Jordan. 'But she didn't believe such a paragon as I described existed.'

'You can believe it,' Joe assured her. 'Here he is in the flesh.'

Looking suitably embarrassed, the ginger-haired young man said, 'Steady on now, or I'll be asking for a rise!' Getting to his feet he engulfed Lyall's fingers in a ham-like fist. 'Patrick Duggan. Pleased to meet you, Mrs Jameson.' He was short and stocky with bright blue eyes and one of the most engaging grins Lyall had ever seen. His accent was pure Cockney.

She smiled warmly at him, liking him on sight, despite anticipating the opposite.

'You look a bit tired, lass,' Joe remarked.

Thrown off balance by this sudden observation, Lyall sought for a light answer. 'Well, I've spent quite a lot of time in bed. I . . .'

'Where else?' murmured Jordan, with a devilish gleam in his amber eyes.

'Where else, indeed?' Joe agreed solemnly.

As Lyall began to blush furiously, all three men burst out laughing.

'Men!' she said witheringly. 'What I was going to say was I slept late most mornings . . .' But it was so wonderful to hear her grandfather laugh that she found herself laughing with them.

'Come and see what Jordan's had done.' Joe sounded pleased as Punch. 'I don't know how he managed it in the time. Oh, and take a look at *this*.' He touched a button on the arm of his wheelchair. Lyall heard the slight whirr of an electric motor and the chair began to move easily. 'Mobile again,' Joe said proudly, 'and under my own steam.'

'That's wonderful!' she cried, and swallowed past the tight knot of tears in her throat.

Joe's three rooms, a pleasant sitting-room with a dining-area and access to the garden, and a comfortable bedroom with an adjoining bathroom, formed a separate unit, with Duggan's rooms at the end. The bathroom had been carefully adapted, with a low bath and special rails and handgrips. Everywhere was painted in cheerful pastel colours. Oh, the power that money could buy to get things done! Though Jordan's revenge wasn't coming cheap,

Lyall thought with bitter humour.

Joe was delighted with everything, and didn't hesitate to sing Jordan's praises. 'You've a man in a million there. But I don't need to tell you that. I could see from the very first how you felt about him, and I was sure you'd marry him.'

'It had nothing to do with his money,' Lyall insisted. 'Nothing.'

Her grandfather looked surprised. 'I never supposed it did, lass. I know you too well to think otherwise . . . By the way, did you manage to scrape enough together to get him that little antique paperweight you mentioned?'

'Yes, I got it, thanks mainly to you.'

'Well, it was worth every penny if it gave him as much pleasure as you thought it would.'

As Joe was clearly waiting for a reply she said, 'Yes . . . Yes, he told me I was very clever . . .' Her voice shook and, afraid she'd let the heartbreak show, she abruptly stopped speaking.

Seeing her emotion, Joe patted her hand. 'It's all right, lass. I know how much you love him.'

While she struggled for control Jordan's voice asked from the doorway, 'Everything all right, Joe? Now you've actually used the new facilities you'll be able to say if anything needs altering.'

'Not a thing,' Joe answered cheerfully. 'I'm doing fine.'

'I've fixed up some full-day physiotherapy, beginning tomorrow,' Jordan announced. 'It should help to ease any pain you're still suffering and hopefully make you a bit more mobile. Duggan should be able to get you and your chair in and out of the new van without too much difficulty . . .'

Not wanting to face Jordan until her armour was safely back in place, Lyall slipped away while he was still talking.

Duggan had vanished and she guessed that tact was one of his many virtues.

She sat in front of the fire and thought that if Jordan had loved her and everything had been all right, it would have seemed like home. But as things were it was merely a prison. A large, luxurious one, but a prison nevertheless.

Lyall had no idea which bedroom she and Jordan would share. Presumably they *would* share, though there must be plenty of rooms. She had only been to the penthouse once before, the night he'd first brought her up there, and she'd never seen over it, but she knew it covered the whole of the top floor.

Her eyelids were drooping and she was half-asleep before Jordan reappeared. His face a smooth mask of politeness, he said, 'I'm sorry, I should have shown you around first, then you could have been taking a nap if you were tired.'

'Oh, no,' she denied, a kind of perverse pride making her reluctant to admit the truth, 'I'm not tired. It's just the heat of the fire.'

'Ready for a quick tour, then?' he suggested.

She got up and followed him like a nicely trained puppy.

While Joe's and Duggan's rooms were at one end of the suite, the well-fitted kitchen and Wilkes's quarters were at the other. Each had its own lift. The main rooms were in the centre, grouped around the foyer. As well as the living-room and two large bedrooms with dressing-rooms and bathrooms en suite, Jordan had a study with book-lined walls. Everywhere was light, with a sense of space and freedom.

Jordan's room, with natural pine units and king-size bed, was decorated in shades of cream and mushroom. It was an attractive, if somewhat severe, décor.

Watching her look around, Jordan said, 'You can have it

redecorated it you don't care for the colour scheme.'

'Aren't you afraid I might choose pink frills?' she asked a shade tartly.

'No,' he answered calmly. 'Though you're one of the most feminine women I've ever known, I don't think pink frills are your style. I would have guessed something grey and green and gold, like an April day.'

How could he know her so well, yet not know her at all?

Their cases were already there, set side by side on a pinewood chest which served as a window seat. 'Shall I unpack for you?' she queried, uncertain of what was expected of her.

'Eager to begin your wifely duties?' A gleam in his eye, Jordan glanced meaningfully at the bed.

Flushing, she turned hurriedly away to open her own case. As she took out her things he stood close by, picking up odd garments and fingering them. Her clothes were all pretty and chosen with care, but they were inexpensive.

'If you're looking for designer labels, you won't find any,' she informed him crisply.

Ignoring the gauntlet, he asked mildly, 'So what do you think of Duggan? Or haven't you had time to make up your mind?'

'I like him,' she admitted honestly. 'And, more important, Grandad likes him.' Which made her prison bars that much stronger. If Joe had seemed in any degree unhappy, she would have felt justified in doing her level best to get both of them away. But as it was, how could she deliberately disrupt something which appeared to be working so well?

Perhaps she sighed, because Jordan said quite gently, 'Why don't you leave the unpacking, and stretch out on the bed for an hour before dinner?' At her quick, alarmed glance he added wryly, 'It's all right, no need to panic, I'm going to the study now to catch up on some work.'

When Lyall had emptied her case, putting her soiled clothes in the laundry basket and everything else neatly away in the plentiful drawers and fitted wardrobes, she decided to follow Jordan's advice. Closing the heavy velvet-lined curtains against the gathering dusk, she took off her shoes and dress and slid beneath the covers. Being so high above the busy street and the streaming traffic, the penthouse was relatively quiet, and she was asleep in a very short time.

She slept for over two hours, and awoke dazed and disorientated. When she had gathered her wits she stood by the window for a while, looking out over the fascinating kaleidoscope of lights to London's skyline, before getting showered and changed.

Having put on a dinner dress in smoky-grey chiffon with a plain round neck and long floating sleeves cut with a simple elegance which disguised the fact that it was 'off the peg', she brushed her hair until it shone, and left it loose.

Jordan only appeared as she was putting the finishing touches to her appearance. He gave her an appreciative look and asked, 'Feeling better?'

'Yes, thank you,' she said politely, and made to go.

'Lyall . . .' His voice halted her. He took a box from his pocket and went on, 'I'd like you to wear this.' Before she could form any protest he had stepped behind her and fastened the emerald necklace around her slender throat.

She put up a hand to touch it. Her first impulse was to refuse to wear it, but perhaps because he'd asked, rather than ordered, she wavered. Added to that was the fact that she hardly felt up to making an issue of it. She let her hand drop again, leaving the necklace where it was.

He smiled, and, recalling how she'd sworn not to wear it, Lyall felt ruffled that he'd won so easily.

She started for the door, but he again stopped her, remarking, 'Your grandfather seems to have settled in very well.'

When she didn't speak he went on slowly, as if choosing his words with care, 'Things need only be as bad as you make them, Lyall.'

'That's strange,' she murmured sweetly. 'I could have sworn you held the whiphand.'

He sighed. 'For Joe's sake, if no one else's . . .'

She broke in sharply. 'Though I've been lured into a marriage that's nothing but a cruel trap, for Grandad's sake I'm willing to pretend I'm ecstatically happy.'

As soon as the words were spoken, Lyall regretted her impulse to lash out at him. But before she could make any attempt to repair the damage, Jordan's face hardened, he turned on his heel and went into the bathroom, closing the door behind him with a decisive snap.

Biting her lips, she cursed her own stupidity. He'd made what seemed to be a genuine attempt to ease the situation, and all she'd done was throw his kindness in his face.

At Jordan's insistence, Duggan joined them for dinner. With Lyall hiding her depression beneath a smile, and Jordan appearing in good spirits, the meal became a festive one. The necklace was much admired, and Lyall, while saying little, did her best to look delighted.

Duggan proved to be excellent company. He had a lively mind and a colourful turn of phrase, and took an equal share in the conversation without ever overstepping his own mark. He was clearly a man who, though not in the least subservient, preferred to keep his place, a man who quietly respected himself and knew his own worth. Very much like Joe, in fact. Perhaps that accounted for the friendship which had sprung up so quickly between the two men, Lyall thought.

When they had had coffee and a leisurely brandy in front of the fire, Duggan said, 'Well, if you don't mind, I think I'll take myself off. There's a programme on the telly I'd like to see.'

Lyall, who had watched him quietly note that Joe was getting very tired, gave him full marks for tact as her grandfather announced, 'If it's snooker, I'll join you. I reckon Taylor should do it without too much trouble.'

'Not on your nelly!' snorted Duggan.

Smiling at the ginger-haired young man, Lyall got up to kiss her grandfather fondly. Then, wrangling amicably, the two departed, Duggan walking alongside the wheelchair.

As she returned to her own seat, sensing what Jordan had in mind, she deliberately chose to go behind his chair rather than in front of it. But he reached a lazy hand over his shoulder and caught hold of her wrist, tilting his head backwards to look at her, before drawing her round the chair and on to his lap.

She sat stiffly erect, holding herself away from him, her spine rigid, her flushed face averted. He eased her back against him and cupped her breast. She could feel the warmth of his hand through the thin material of her dress. When his thumb began to stroke caressingly over the sensitive nipple, she said in a stifled voice, 'Don't . . . please don't.'

He took not the slightest notice of her plea. All evening she had sensed the simmering anger he was concealing beneath an urbane mask. Now she shivered, sure the devil in him was intent on making her pay for her earlier hasty words. Fear made her lose her cool. With a sudden jerk she freed herself and, jumping up, rounded on him. 'I said don't touch me! I *hate* you to touch me!'

'Just at the moment,' he said slowly, 'I don't much care what your feelings are. I want you, and I intend to have you.'

Lyall's face went paper-pale and, recoiling, she ran for the bedroom. She was able to close the door and turn the key in the lock before he reached it. Breathing fast, she leaned limply against the panels. The door handle turned, sending her heart into her mouth. But when there was no further sound or movement she relaxed slightly. He might be furious, but he could hardly start breaking down the door with so many people close at hand.

She was just straightening up with a feeling of reprieve when he strolled casually in from the adjoining dressing-room. Shock almost stopped her breath. Fool! She'd stupidly forgotten that the smaller room had another door.

'Having fun?' he asked caustically.

'Leave me alone,' she choked, as he came towards her. Then, in desperation, 'Suppose I get pregnant?'

'We're married,' he pointed out. 'And if you do have my child, my hold on you will only be stronger.'

'I hate you,' she muttered fiercely.

'So I gather.' Jordan sounded unconcerned. 'That being the case, what have I got to lose?'

'Nothing,' she said, fighting back now with every weapon she could find. 'Nothing at all, if your self-respect can stand it and you don't mind the idea of rape.'

There was silence for a moment or two, then he said evenly, 'But I do.'

'Well, rape is what it will be. I'll fight tooth and nail.'

'Pity. Tonight I'd rather hoped to have your co-operation. Your *active* co-operation.'

Lyall shook her head. 'I won't let you seduce me.'

He looked at her, taking in the dark, silky hair, the green, heavy-lashed eyes tilting upwards slightly at the corners, the small, straight nose above a neatly rounded chin, the soft mouth now set in a determined line, and said thoughtfully, 'Well, I could put that statement to the test . . . But, as it's still quite early, suppose we play a game, with a prize for the winner.'

'A game?' she said warily. 'What kind of game?'

'Chess.' He pursed his lips thoughtfully. 'You do play chess, don't you?'

It was on the tip of her tongue to say no, when she remembered he already knew the answer. 'Grandad taught me,' she admitted shortly. 'But I'm a poor player. I don't really have the brains.'

'Now *that* I doubt. Still, if you don't want to play . . .' He gave her a challenging look.

As levelly as possible she asked, 'What kind of prize had you in mind?'

Amused by her caution, he said, 'If you win I'll move into the dressing-room and tonight you can sleep alone.'

Her heart lifted with hope, then as quickly fell, as she began to see where this was leading. Carefully, she said, 'And I suppose if you win you'll want my . . . co-operation?'

'Oh, a little more than that, I think. If I win *you* can make love to *me*. Scared?' he taunted when she blanched.

If she refused to play, he'd probably take her to bed anyway, but if she agreed she would have some chance of winning. Making up her mind, and seeing an opportunity to get a few days' reprieve, she said boldly, 'If I win, I want to sleep alone for the rest of the week.'

'You drive a hard bargain,' he teased.

'Will you agree to that?' she insisted.

'Very well.' With a flourish, Jordan indicated she should precede him back to the living-room.

Unlocking the door, she did so.

When he'd thrown a couple of logs on the fire he went to the sideboard and found a folding chessboard and a box of pieces. Golden eyes gleaming, he set them out on the coffee-table. 'And to give you some small advantage, you can have white,' he told her smoothly.

Her dark, glossy head bent over the black and white board, the shadow of her long lashes lying on her cheeks, the tip of a pink tongue protruding in concentration, Lyall tried to use every ounce of skill she possessed. Watching each move, she played a careful, defensive game, avoiding the traps he set for her, refusing his many tempting ploys, giving nothing away.

He played a fast, attacking game, as she might have expected, and sacrificed several good pieces. Then he made a bad mistake and, hardly daring to believe her luck, she took his queen.

Emboldened by his discomfort, and remembering how her grandfather had always insisted that attack was the best means of defence, she had just moved to corner his king when he castled and escaped.

She was moving to attack from another position when all at once she found herself in trouble, her king in check. Desperately she cast around for an escape route and found none.

Softly, triumphantly, Jordan said, 'Checkmate, I think.'

The defeat was as bitter on her tongue as Dead Sea apples. Jordan had been clever, playing with her, letting her believe she had him on the run, while all the time he'd been poised for the kill.

Forcing down the futile anger, Lyall squared her shoulders and said, as evenly as possible, 'I knew I was no good at chess. I should have stuck out for poker.'

He saluted her spirit and held out an imperious hand. Like someone who had no will of their own, she put hers into it.

Pulling her on to his knee, he settled back comfortably and, removing his tie, coiled it neatly before unfastening the top two buttons of his shirt. Then, his gold-flecked eyes on her face, he waited, giving her no further help.

For the first time she considered the price she was going to have to pay for losing. 'You make love to me,' he'd said. If things had been different it would have seemed only too easy, a lovers' game. Now it was the hardest thing she had ever attempted in her life.

'Don't look so distraught!' he mocked. 'Even though you'd never gone the whole way you must have played this little scene many times before, led your would-be lovers on. Men don't give expensive gifts without encouragement. Pretend you're trying to coax a diamond bracelet out of me. You might even manage it. God knows, you're enticing enough . . .'

With an incoherent murmur of rage Lyall tore herself free, but in a couple of paces he caught her, pulling her down on the rug with him. 'Well, if you're still determined to dissemble, pretend a little, make believe I'm the love of your life.'

She closed her eyes for a moment, his derisive words burning into her soul like acid.

'Or do you plan to chicken out of our bargain?'

'No, I don't,' she flashed.

'Then kiss me, touch me.'

Tentatively she lifted a hand and touched his cheek,

brushing her fingertips over the beautifully chiselled mouth to trace the cleft in his chin. It was what she'd always wanted to do, she admitted at last. She'd longed to touch him. Her heart began to beat with an erratic, jerky movement that made her breathing quicken . . .

If she closed her mind to everything, and pretended that he loved her, that their marriage was real, holding out a promise of delight for the present and contentment for the future, then she *could* keep her half of the bargain.

Her fingers stroked down the warm, strong column of his neck and slipped inside his shirt. His skin was smooth and exciting to touch. Bending her head, she brushed her lips against his.

Still he made no move to help her, and daringly she nipped his lower lip between her pearly teeth. It was innocently provocative. With a low growl he came to life, and his hand spread across the back of her head to hold her mouth against his. Her lips parted invitingly and he deepened the kiss until she took fire.

He began to co-operate then, removing his own clothes and hers. There was an urgency in his movements and she knew he was burning as she was. Putting up her hands, she tried to unfasten the emerald necklace which was lying heavy against her warm skin.

'Leave it,' said Jordan thickly. 'It looks wonderful.'

Lying back on the rug, he pulled her down beside him. She lifted herself away a little and ran a teasing fingertip from his chest to the flat, taut stomach. Feeling the instant jerk of his response, she knew a heady excitement.

With a groan he caught her hand and held it away from him. She tugged it free and, lost to everything but her own need to touch and feel and explore, ran it over his muscular ribcage and up to follow the line of his collarbone.

Abruptly she realised that the smooth, lightly tanned skin of his right shoulder was marred by purple marks. For a second or two she stared blankly at the dark bruising, until it occurred to her that he must have done it the previous day when he'd broken out of the storeroom.

With a soft murmur of contrition she touched his shoulder with her fingertips and, her face full of an overwhelming tenderness, bent to kiss the bruises.

He sat up with a movement so sudden it took her completely unawares, and thrust her roughly away from him. She tumbled over and, dazed and bewildered, slowly picked herself up. 'W-what's the matter?' she stammered. 'What's wrong?'

'Damn you for a deceitful little bitch!' he snarled. Then, his face twisted with fury, he ordered, 'Go on, get out of my sight!'

CHAPTER EIGHT

For endless seconds Lyall stared at him numbly, her lovely eyes stricken. Then, as red, mortified colour poured into her face, she turned on her heel and fled.

Her breath coming in little gasps, she scrambled into bed and, her knees drawn up, huddled beneath the covers in a protective ball. What had she done? Why had Jordan rejected her so brutally? Was it just another way of humiliating her? Another form of punishment?

He'd said, 'You make love to me. Kiss me, touch me . . .' And she'd done what he asked. She'd wiped from her consciousness all the misery and anguish of the past few days and thought only that he was her husband, the man she had fallen so hopelessly in love with. All feeling of coercion had quickly vanished, and she'd found herself lost in a world of sensual delight, wanting only to give and receive pleasure. Wanting to show all the love she'd kept hidden. But he'd thrust her away as if she disgusted him . . .

As she hid her burning face in the pillow she felt the movement at her throat, and fumbled to remove the necklace which weighed now like some shackle. Its safety catch defeated her, and she was forced to leave it where it was.

A long time seemed to elapse before Jordan came to bed. When he eventually got in beside her, though he lay still and apparently relaxed, Lyall could sense his restlessness.

His body had been intensely stimulated; it was his mind

that had rejected her. Lying there in the gloom, she wondered bleakly if he would just use her to assuage his frustration and allow him to sleep. But his self-control held. He made no move to touch her, and she felt his mind would always dominate his flesh. He was still lying awake when finally she fell asleep.

Lyall came to, slowly, reluctantly, to find Jordan sitting on the bed. He was showered and shaved and dressed in a well-cut business suit. She struggled to sit up, pushing back her cloud of hair. He was staring at her, and she saw the flame ignite in his tawny eyes. Even so, it was a moment or two before she appreciated she was naked apart from the necklace. With a convulsive movement she pulled the covers up to her chin.

'Do you intend to keep wearing that bauble?' he asked.

'No, I . . . I couldn't unfasten it.'

'Let me.'

She lowered the covers very slightly, keeping a grip on the edges.

Anger tightened his mouth. With a swift yank he dragged them down to her waist. 'I'm your husband. Don't try to hide yourself from me.'

Gritting her teeth, she bent her head while he unfastened the necklace and dropped it into his pocket, as if it were the bauble he'd called it.

Seeing her shiver slightly, he reached for her négligé and put it around her shoulders, before saying casually, 'I have a lot to do today. I hope you can amuse yourself until this evening? Unfortunately they slipped up on your car. I ordered a nice little white Porsche to be waiting for you, but they delivered the wrong model, and Wilkes took it upon himself to send it back. They say it will take another day or two to get the model I wanted, but they're hoping to have one here before the weekend. I imagine you'd like your own transport as soon as possible?'

Astonished and confused, Lyall stayed silent.

Jordan glanced at her and reading her expression accurately said, 'Surely you didn't think I intended to keep you a virtual prisoner?'

She *had* thought that.

'You don't look very pleased that I'm not,' he commented. 'Or is it that you'd prefer some other make of car?'

'N-no,' she stammered. 'Of course not. It's just that I . . . I . . .' She faltered to a halt. What she wanted to tell him was that she would happily forsake anything his money could buy, if only he didn't believe she was a mercenary tramp and hold her responsible for Paul's death, but the words wouldn't come. Instead she said unsteadily, 'I'm just overwhelmed, that's all. I . . . I don't know what to say.'

'You needn't say anything. But you could try giving me a thank-you kiss.'

Reluctantly she brushed cool lips across the smooth cheek that smelled of some tangy aftershave.

'Is that the best you can do?' he scoffed.

'I don't understand you,' she protested helplessly. 'Last night you asked me to kiss you, and when I did . . .' Her voice broke.

'Yes, the way I treated you was hardly fair,' he admitted heavily. 'But just at that minute I was sickened by your falseness.'

'Falseness?' she echoed. 'I don't know what you mean.'

'You know well enough. That look of love on your face when you touched me. The tenderness when you kissed my shoulder . . . How did you make those emotions appear so real, Lyall?'

She lifted her head and looked at him, her eyes sparkling brilliant as emeralds. 'You said yourself that I was a good actress.'

'Yes,' he agreed with a touch of bitterness, 'so I did.' Getting to his feet, he strode away, leaving her staring after him, hurt and bereft.

If only she could hate him. She *wanted* to hate him. Hating him would be preferable to the pain of this one-sided loving.

When she had managed to regain her equilibrium, Lyall showered and dressed and, as soon as she'd put on some make-up, went to say good morning to Joe. She found him propped up on his pillows, freshly shaven, his grizzled hair neatly combed, tucking into a substantial breakfast while he read the morning paper.

'I don't need to ask if you're all right,' she said fondly, stooping to kiss his cheek.

'I'm getting thoroughly spoilt,' he told her with his old boyish grin.

'What would you like to do today?' she asked.

He shook his head at her. 'This is still officially your honeymoon. In any case, today is the first of my clinic days. Duggan is taking me over to Nathan Road for a full session of physiotherapy.'

'Oh yes, of course.' Jordan had mentioned it the previous day. So what was she to do with herself? Lyall wondered forlornly. Mitch would be at work . . .

A tap interrupted her thoughts and Duggan came in. He gave her his infectious grin and said, 'Morning, Mrs Jameson. How do you think he's looking?'

'Marvellous,' she replied brightly. 'And I understand you're off to the clinic to add to the good work.'

'Yes, that's right.' He ran a hand through his red hair. 'It's one of those days I could do with being in two places at once.'

'When he can, Duggan helps out at St Thomas's Centre, a mission in the East End,' Joe explained. 'And it seems they could do with him today. Not as a nurse, but for his cooking skills.'

'What kind of mission is it?' asked Lyall.

Duggan answered. 'A private one. They run a small hostel, and a kitchen to supply the homeless with food. In weather like this, a hot meal can mean the difference between life and death to someone living rough.'

Lyall's interest was aroused. 'How do they manage? Where does the money come from?'

'Why, a great deal of it from . . .' Duggan stopped short, then went on, 'Well, various sources, most of it donated by private individuals, and all the work is done by unpaid volunteers. As you can imagine, the regular staff are quite often shorthanded. But the problem at the moment is, there's no one to do the cooking, Mrs Simpson, the regular cook has slipped on some ice and hurt her knee. Amy O'Brian, the woman in charge, rang to see if I could help out for a few days, but . . .'

'Tell you what,' suggested Joe, 'I could always skip the clinic and . . .'

'Oh no, you couldn't.' Duggan vetoed that suggestion immediately. 'Mr Jameson would have my guts for garters!'

'He's gone out and won't be back until this evening,' Lyall told him.

Duggan shook his head. 'It wouldn't be right. This is the job I'm being paid to do.'

'Well, if Jordan's not in,' said Joe, 'perhaps Lyall could go with me.'

'It really needs a man,' Duggan objected. 'I mean, from the strength angle. Mrs Jameson would never manage all that has to be done.'

'Well, I'll tell you what I could do.' Lyall felt a growing excitement. 'I could stand in for your cook.'

Both men stared at her. Then Joe agreed, 'You could that, lass.' To Duggan, he said proudly, 'Lyall is as good a cook as her grandmother was.'

'But Mrs Jameson couldn't . . .'

'Of course I could,' Lyall interrupted firmly. The sooner she could establish some normal life, the better. 'It will give me something to do while . . . while Jordan's at the office. I wouldn't want to just sit in all day. I'm used to working.'

'Well, if you're sure?' Duggan still sounded doubtful. 'It's very hard work.'

'I'm quite sure. All I need to know is how to get there and who to report to.'

'I can drop you at St Thomas's before we go to the clinic, and pick you up again at four.' Duggan sounded enthusiastic now. 'You report to Amy O'Brian, and she'll tell you everything you need to know. By the way, it gets very hot in the kitchen even in this weather, so you'll need to dress in something light. Oh, and it wouldn't be wise to go wearing that.' He nodded at her engagement ring.

'Oh . . .'

As she hesitated, wondering where to leave such a valuable thing, he suggested, 'Wilkes could put it in the safe for you.'

Lyall smiled her relief and went to find the manservant.

A short while later, a lightweight skirt and blouse beneath her outdoor things, she climbed into the specially adapted cream van with the two men, and sat in the rear by Joe's wheelchair.

Within half an hour they dropped her in a seedy area, where the terraced houses were little better than slums and a bitter wind blew litter along the narrow streets. She stood outside the crumbling Victorian building, which had once been a school, and waved them off before going in to introduce herself to Miss O'Brian.

That good lady was ensconced in a dark area just off the main entrance, which had once been cloakrooms. It now served as an overcrowded office-cum-storeroom. When Lyall had given her name and explained briefly why she was there, Miss O'Brian, or Amy, as she preferred to be called, was first surprised, then delighted.

She was a gaunt, grey-haired woman with the staying power of a marathon runner and the driving force of a tank. She'd found her vocation in caring for God's poor lost souls and, her pale eyes glowing with the enthusiasm of the truly dedicated, followed it unswervingly.

'So Patrick sent you,' she cried. 'Sure, the man's a marvel! Well now, there's no time to lose if we're to start serving at twelve. Fiona and Liz have turned up, thank the good Lord. They'll do the potatoes and vegetables if you can cope with the rest? The menu should be steak and kidney pie and treacle pudding.'

'Fine,' said Lyall cheerfully. 'Do you know how many for?'

'Until the food runs out,' Amy answered with devastating practicality. 'Now come and have a look at the kitchen, and I'll show you where everything is.'

The cooking facilities, though antiquated, were spotlessly clean. There were two large stone sinks with a potato-peeling machine, and ovens, friers, a huge steamer and several coppers were arranged back to back in an oblong in the centre of the red quarry-tiled floor.

Various other machines, for mixing pastry, and so on, were set between the working surfaces. A narrow pantry stored dry items and tinned stuff, while a tall, old-fashioned fridge held the fresh food. Beneath the windows at the far end were sinks for washing up, and the long middle wall had three hatches which opened into what had once been the old school hall.

As soon as she'd finished the brisk tour, Amy went hurrying off, her faith in her new cook's ability to cope gratifying. And it wouldn't be misplaced, Lyall decided firmly.

Though she was used to cooking, she'd never before done it on such a large scale but, using the mixing machine to make batch after batch of pastry, she soon had the ovens filled with trays of pie. Wiping the sweat from her face with the corner of the white cotton overall she'd donned, she made a start on the treacle puddings.

The two helpers—Fiona, young, thin, blonde, zealous, and obviously 'upper class', Liz, middle-aged, plump, with dyed hair and bad feet, and obviously lonely—stopped to have a coffee and a bite to eat about eleven-thirty. Lyall joined them for a quick drink, then carried on coping with the temperamental steamer as best she could.

When it was full of puddings and hissing away venomously, she mixed dried milk, cornflour and flavourings, and made a copper full of custard, stirring it with an implement the size of a canoe paddle.

Just after twelve, the middle hatch was opened and, from cooking, Lyall turned to dishing up the food. The three women worked side by side, serving heaped plates to what seemed to be a never-ending, shuffling queue.

Lyall's soft heart was pierced by the pathetic miscellany of men and women, young and old, drunks and junkies, vagrants and drifters, drop-outs and misfits, the pitiful dregs of a largely uncaring society. It seemed to her they all had two things in common. The first, a crying need for a hot meal to keep body and soul together; the second, an air of detachment, as if they had rejected—and been rejected by—their fellow men. Seeing so many human beings in such dire straits was a salutary experience which pretty soon cut her own troubles down to size.

The day fairly flew past, and by the time the men came to collect her she was bone-weary, but satisfied that she'd done what little she could. After assuring a relieved Amy that she would be there next day, Lyall climbed into the van for the return journey.

'Everything go all right?' Duggan wanted to know as he drove through the tea-time traffic.

'We managed to feed everyone who came,' she answered slowly. 'But I was shocked by the number of people who need help. I had no idea . . .'

'A lot of folks haven't,' he told her. 'More's the pity.'

Turning to her grandfather, who was looking tired but quietly jubilant, Lyall asked, 'So how did you get on?'

'Fine. I had a massage and some heat treatment on my back, then after lunch I actually went in the pool.' For the rest of the way back he talked enthusiastically about plans for future sessions.

As she listened, Lyall couldn't help but think how different it would have been if he'd had to stay cooped up all day in a cramped flat just waiting for her to come home from work. Jordan had done so much for her grandfather, a lot of things he needn't have done. The least she could do was thank him.

After a relaxing soak in a hot bath, she changed into a pretty floral dress, put on her make-up and waited with a mixture of emotions for him to come home.

When seven o'clock arrived and there was still no sign of him, Lyall, at Wilkes's suggestion, joined her grandfather and Duggan for the evening meal. So Joe wouldn't worry, she put on a cheerful face and said, 'I expect he's still hard at it. He once told me, when he was at work nothing else existed.'

Joe grunted. 'You should have stayed in the Lakes, lass.'

As soon as dinner was over, Lyall kissed Joe, bade Duggan goodnight, and returned to the main living-room. She switched on the television, but a weak comedy failed to hold her interest, and so did the book she borrowed from the well-stocked shelves.

Where *was* Jordan? Surely he wasn't still working at ten o'clock at night? If only he'd come home, she felt she could talk to him, at least tell him how very grateful she was for all he was doing for her grandfather; though she still felt some bitterness and resentment at the way *she'd* been treated, she *was* grateful.

She sighed. There had been times when Jordan had seemed to soften, odd moments when, despite everything, they had seemed close. Surely, as he really got to know her, he would realise she wasn't the kind of woman he thought her? Lulled by the warmth of the flickering fire, Lyall allowed herself to hope, to dream . . .

It was well after eleven when Jordan got home, and she was curled on the settee, dozing. The click of the latch brought her head up and she blinked at him, her eyes sleepy, her cheeks pink.

'I met some friends and had a meal with them,' he said. Adding with a glint, 'But if I'd known you were waiting up for me . . .' He tossed his jacket over a chair and came to sit by her. Feeling at a disadvantage lying down, she moved hastily to put her feet on the floor and sit up.

'How did Joe's physiotherapy go?' he queried, when he'd watched her manoeuvre with mocking eyes.

She told him all her grandfather had said, then went on, 'I want to thank you for everything that you're doing for Grandad. You're very kind.'

His head jerked a little, as if her innocent words were a rock she'd hit him with, and she glimpsed discomfort that was almost pain in his tawny eyes. Then his guard was up again and he was asking a shade curtly, 'How did you spend your day? I hope you weren't bored?'

Lyall hesitated before admitting, 'Well, Duggan had a phone call from a Miss O'Brian, who runs a mission in the East End . . .'

Jordan sat in silence, his expression shuttered, while she told him about St Thomas's. Uncertain how he had taken it, she went on, 'I'm going again tomorrow . . . I hope you don't mind?'

'Why should I mind, if that's how you want to fill your days? The thing that puzzles me is why, when you don't have to work, you choose to go and slave there.'

'Well, they needed a cook and I needed to do something to pass the time. I don't think I'm cut out to be a lady of leisure. And it's a job that's well worth doing,' Lyall added a shade defensively.

Shaking his head almost in disbelief, he said slowly, 'You are the most surprising woman. Nothing about you seems to add up.'

Lyall felt a spark of hope kindle. Was he beginning to have doubts? Wonder if he might have been wrong about her? Impulsively she put a hand on his arm. 'Perhaps it's because you're not starting with right set of figures.'

As if her light touch brought him to life, he captured her hand and used it to draw her closer. 'I know one figure that's not merely right, it's quite perfect,' he told her softly, and watched her eyes turn to deepest jade, the black pupils grow even larger.

His fingers, lean and very masculine against the pastel colours of her dress, moved to mould one of her slender shoulders, before slipping lower to cup a breast surprisingly full for so slight a girl. She shivered as his other hand went to caress the nape of her neck.

As if hypnotised, she gazed into that strong face so close to hers. A disturbing face, handsome as Lucifer, with its heavy-lashed, gold-flecked eyes, its cleft chin and beautiful, sensitive mouth. Light-headed and giddy, as if she'd drunk too much wine, she swayed towards him, her eyes closing, her lips parted for his kiss.

When his mouth brushed hers, she breathed a small sigh, but, instead of deepening the kiss, he took her chin and gave her head a little shake. 'Don't close your eyes,' he ordered huskily. 'You have the most fascinating eyes I've ever seen on a woman. Expressive eyes. I want to look into them and see what you're feeling while I make love to you.'

Her eyes flew open and her intoxication died as swiftly as

if it had been guillotined, leaving her stone-cold sober. He wanted to strip her of any protection, to leave her naked and vulnerable, to look into her very soul. If he'd cared about her it would have been an affirmation of her love, an act of faith. But he didn't.

The stinging pain this thought brought made her want to hit back. 'Make love?' she echoed bitterly. 'Is that what you call it? Why don't you at least be honest and admit that love is the last thing it is? It's revenge, punishment, humiliation, lust . . .'

Jordan's lips thinned. 'Your humiliation and my lust, you mean?'

'Yes,' she cried recklessly, 'that's exactly what I mean!'

'So be it,' he said harshly. Getting to his feet, he swept her up into his arms and carried her to the bedroom. Setting her down on the bed with care, he slipped off her shoes and, his face intent, began to undress her.

Her eyes dry, her heart full of anguish, Lyall lay limp as a rag doll while he removed her dress and lacy bra, but when he ran a caressing hand over her breasts she couldn't repress a shiver.

'Like that?' he asked.

'I *hate* it. I *hate* you to touch me,' she said in a stifled voice.

He merely smiled and finished stripping her, savouring every moment. When she lay naked, he sat on the edge of the bed looking down at her, his eyes travelling appreciatively over the slim curves of her body. Then his hand followed his eyes, sliding down the creamy skin of her flat belly to gently tug one of the short dark curls of glossy hair.

When she still lay unmoving, he smiled again, as if amused by her passive resistance, and leaving her lying there stood up to strip off his own clothing.

As he started to remove his shirt, Lyall's eyes were drawn to the masculine beauty of that strong, lithe body. Powerful muscles rippled beneath the smooth skin, which had kept its golden tan even in winter, and small, flat nipples broke the wide expanse of chest. A haze of dark, curly hair tapered downwards past his lean waist and disappeared into the top of his trousers. Her throat went tight and she tried not to look as his hands went to the clip and zipper at his waistband.

Once he was naked, he bent to lift her further into the middle of the large bed before sliding in beside her. Though her heart was flapping about like a stranded fish and it was difficult to breathe, she forced herself to lie quite still.

He took her chin, and, turning her face towards him studied her blank, closed look. Then he laughed. 'Oh, no, that won't work,' he told her mocking. 'You won't stop me that way.'

His face moved nearer; his tawny eyes came into sharp focus, then blurred as he bent his head. Shutting her eyes tightly, Lyall took a deep breath and braced herself for his assault.

Perhaps he'd intended to take her roughly, but somehow it didn't turn out that way. Maybe her lack of resistance swayed him, but whatever the reason, when he kissed her it was with a totally unexpected sweetness that was as heady as champagne.

His mouth gentled hers, not forcing but coaxing and teasing her lips to part for him. When they did, he kissed her deeply, druggingly, while his hands moved over her slender warmth almost reverently, as if she was some exquisite but fragile treasure he enjoyed touching.

'You're so lovely,' he murmured. 'Your skin feels like

silk. I want to kiss every inch of it.'

Suiting the action to the words, his mouth followed his hands over her scented flesh, the tip of his tongue touching, tasting, electrifying every nerve-ending, making her gasp and tremble.

She tried to resist, tried to exert will-power over flesh, but her nipples firmed and a moist heat of desire began to throb, making soft little whimpers form in her throat. Her brain clouded and all she was conscious of was the man and the need he had aroused in her. It flooded her entire being, engulfed and swept her away.

Ravishment.

Jordan knew he had won long before he moved over her, and victory was sweet. He took her gasps of shuddering ecstasy into his mouth, enjoying them with the fierce delight of a conqueror.

Roused to fever-pitch, he made love to her several times before, temporarily sated, he rolled, taking her with him so she lay against the hard length of his body, her head on his chest.

She was briefly aware of his heart thundering beneath her cheek, but, completely devastated, she was deeply asleep long before it quietened and slowed to its normal rate.

When Lyall surfaced she felt a deep physical contentment. Lazily relaxed, she lay for a while drifting, half-asleep and half-awake, enjoying the sensation of warmth and security. Then, as she started to stretch, she realised the warmth was Jordan's body curved around hers as they lay spoon-fashion. His arm was over her ribcage holding her, his hand possessively cupping her breast, his breath lightly ruffling her hair.

If he'd loved her, and theirs had been a normal marriage, she could have turned into his arms to smile at him, give and receive a morning kiss, to perhaps touch him and stir him into desire again.

Shocked, her mind tried to reject the direction her thoughts were taking, but honesty forced her to admit that the more he ravished her body, like some insatiable entity, the more it craved for him. She shivered.

'Cold?' he asked, and his hand left her breast to pull the covers higher around them.

She had stiffened at the sound of his voice, believing him to be asleep. Now she felt the urge to pull herself free, to move away from such intimate contact. But, nervous suddenly of arousing either his temper or his passion, she lay still and tense.

His hand returned to her breast and squeezed gently.

Lyall made a small choked sound of protest.

'Of course—I forgot. You hate me to touch you.' His tone was light and bantering.

She remained silent, biting her lip.

He nuzzled aside her hair and brushed her nape with his lips and tongue-tip. 'Would you like to show me just how much you hate it?'

The certain knowledge that she'd be unable to hide her body's wanton eagerness threw her into a panic. She fought free of his arms, and felt a mixture of relief and disappointment when he let her go easily, without a struggle.

Idly, he turned on to his back to watch her pull on her robe and hurry into the cream and apricot bathroom.

When she returned freshly showered, her teeth cleaned and her hair brushed into a silky cloud around her shoulders, he was lying indolently, his hands clasped behind his dark, curly head.

To hide the rush of feeling the sight of him lying there provoked, she asked tartly, 'Do you plan to stay in bed all day?'

'It depends on how much co-operation I get,' he told her with a wicked grin. 'Were you thinking of coming back?'

'No, I wasn't,' she said thickly.

He sighed. 'Then I might as well get up. But first come and give me a kiss.'

Lyall hesitated, half attracted by, half wary of, this playful mood, but *wanting* to kiss him.

Little devils of mischief dancing in his gold-flecked eyes, Jordan started to sit up, coaxing, 'Come on, just one.'

Approaching the bed cautiously, she bent over.

With a sudden lunge he caught her wrist and, as she gave a startled squeak, pulled her down into his arms, laughing triumphantly. Holding her cradled like a baby, he kissed her not once, but several times, leaving her quivering and breathless. Then, growling deep in his throat, he nuzzled aside the flimsy material of her robe to find the warm softness of her breasts. His chin was rough with stubble and, finding it unbearably erotic, she wriggled and squirmed. He merely held her tighter.

She had just abandoned herself to the blazing excitement when he let her go and, a hand spread against her spine, pushed her upright. 'Ah, well, I did say *one* kiss.' He got out of bed and headed naked for the bathroom.

A few seconds later she heard the shower start to run. Her breath still coming fast and, seething with conflicting emotions, she hurried over her dressing so she could be gone before he returned.

He joined her at the breakfast table quite quickly, dressed in a grey suit with a pale ivory shirt and matching tie. The lazy, laughing-eyed man was gone, in his place a brisk businessman. He helped himself to bacon and eggs while Lyall poured coffee for them both. She found herself resenting that, while she was still quivering inside like a jelly, he could be so calm and unruffled, so obviously unmoved.

'I'm bringing some guests home for dinner tonight,' he remarked as he began to eat. 'Of course, you don't have to worry; Wilkes will take care of everything.'

'How many guests?' She felt suddenly nervous.

'Two, both Americans. Bruce Mantell, who owns a fashion house, and his chief designer. They're in London on business.'

'I suppose you got to know them while you were over there?' Lyall asked.

Jordan nodded. 'I made some very good friends. Life in the States can be most enjoyable.'

'It's a pity you had to come back.' It was just an idle remark, made without thinking, but the change in Jordan was immediate and violent.

Pushing his plate away, he said harshly, 'It's a pity I ever went. If I hadn't, Paul might still be alive.'

'Do you really think you could have altered things?' Her green eyes were intense.

'I'm damned sure I could,' he said forcefully.

'In that case *I* wish you'd never gone. Or at least come home sooner.'

His face whitened. 'Yes, there you have it. I should have come back sooner. When I first realised he was getting desperate over you, losing his grip, I should have come back then.' His dark head bent, he might have been speaking to himself as he went on, 'I was supposed to be looking after him. Dear God, I'm as much to blame for his death as you are.' There was anger and guilt and pain in his voice, a bitterness that seemed to be eating into him like acid.

All at once she saw clearly how it was. Jordan had been the strong one, a self-appointed guardian to the younger, weaker man, and, blaming himself for failing Paul, he had made her a scapegoat, a whipping-boy to vent his futile anger on.

Now, understanding, the bitterness and passionate resentment she'd felt at the way he'd treated her drained away, leaving only sadness. All she could feel for him was an overwhelming sympathy and compassion.

Perhaps neither of them was totally free from blame, but surely Jordan had set himself an impossible task?

'Can any man be his brother's keeper?'

Lyall hardly realised she had spoken the words aloud until he asked wearily, 'Don't you see the mark of Cain?'

Her heart was torn for him. 'No,' she denied strongly. 'You can't feel responsible for what happened.'

For a moment his tawny eyes looked startled, then bleakly he said, 'Can't I? Do you know where I was when Paul needed me? When he died? I was on vacation. Holidaying with my mistress.'

That would be the blonde in the snapshot. The woman named Nancy.

Lyall's hands clenched. 'That's not a crime. You couldn't have known what was going to happen.'

As if he felt the need to unburden himself now he'd started, he went on, 'We were in a log cabin in Vermont, right away from civilisation. Our only contact with people was meeting another couple camping half a mile away. I didn't hear of Paul's death until I got back to New York and it was too late. Oh, God, I wish . . .' Head bent, he broke off abruptly.

Lyall felt a fierce urge to protect him from the pain she could tell was tearing him apart. Lifting his hand, she held it against her cheek. 'With hindsight, there's always something we wish we'd done or not done, and feel guilty about. But I don't believe you could have altered a thing. You didn't see Paul those last few months. He wasn't . . . rational.'

Jordan looked at her then, his gold-hazel eyes brilliant. 'It's strange for you to be giving comfort.'

Steadily she said, 'Not so strange. I know what it feels like to need it. I also know it's no use blaming yourself for what happened to Paul.'

'So I'm to lay all the blame at your door?'

She shook her head. 'Not all of it. Some. I should never have accepted his gifts, and I should have realised how strongly he felt about me and tried to do something about it sooner. I'll always feel guilty about those. But I'm not the callous bitch you make me out to be.'

While she'd been speaking she had unconsciously kept gripping his hand. Now he reversed the position and, raising her hand, put his lips to the palm. 'Lyall, I . . .'

A knock interrupted his words, and Duggan's ginger head was poked round the door. 'About ready to go, Mrs Jameson? I thought if it's OK by you I could run you over to St Thomas's while your grandfather's reading his newspaper.'

'Yes, of course.' Lyall hid her disappointment with a smile and added, 'Give me a couple of minutes.'

As the head was withdrawn, Wilkes came through the opposite door to clear away the breakfast dishes.

Jordan muttered something beneath his breath, then aloud said, 'I must be off. I should get back home no later than seven. Don't overtire yourself.' He dropped a quick, hard kiss on her lips and was gone, leaving her in a turmoil, her heart beating fast with excitement and a growing hope that the difficult relationship between them might really be improving.

CHAPTER NINE

When Lyall had pulled herself together enough, she went along to see Joe, who was still in bed, looking cheerful but a bit tired. He assured her he was fine, then out of the blue asked, 'But what about you? Is everything all right between you and Jordan?'

Trying not to show how much his question had startled her, she laughed and said, 'Just because he was working late, you surely don't . . .'

'No, it's not only that,' Joe broke in. 'Somehow you don't seem really happy.'

Buoyed up by her new-found hope, she managed to say convincingly, 'Whatever put that idea into your head? Of course I'm happy.'

'You do love him, don't you?' persisted Joe.

She nodded. 'If he hadn't a penny to his name I'd follow him barefoot to the ends of the earth if he asked me to.'

Reassured, Joe said cheerily, 'Though Jordan, being the man he is, wouldn't stay penniless for long.'

Duggan was waiting for her in the van and, as she approached, got out to open her door. They talked companionably on the way, and when they reached St Thomas's he went in with her to say hello to Amy.

She greeted them enthusiastically, then, turning to Duggan said, 'You're a miracle worker, so you are. I don't know how we'd have managed without Mrs . . .' She hesitated, before shaking her head. 'I always had difficulty remembering names, but I'm getting a mind like a sieve in my old age.'

'Mrs Jameson,' Duggan supplied. 'I'd have thought you'd have remembered *that* name . . . Well, see you about four.' He gave them a brisk salute and departed, whistling.

'Mrs *Jameson*?' Amy sounded thunderstruck.

'I'm sorry,' Lyall apologised. 'I think yesterday I must have introduced myself as Lyall Summers. You see, I've only been married a short time and I still haven't got used to . . .'

'You're married to Jordan Jameson!' cried Amy. 'Would you credit that, now! Well, he deserves the very best. That man's next door to a saint, so he is. The centre would have closed down long ago if it hadn't been for him.'

'You mean he helps financially?'

'I mean he practically supports it.'

Lyall felt dazed. When she'd talked about the mission, Jordan had given no sign that he'd even heard of the place. But didn't that fit in with what she knew of his character? He was the last man to blow his own trumpet.

Amy was going on, 'And he's not above lending a hand with the chores. Last year, when the centre got flooded, he worked alongside us mopping up and refurbishing the place. Men like him are very few and far between, so they are . . .' It was a good few minutes before she finished singing Jordan's praises.

The day absolutely raced by. In no time at all, it seemed, Duggan was back to pick Lyall up. On the way home she asked the question that had been puzzling her. 'Why didn't you tell me Jordan helps with the upkeep of the mission?'

Duggan glanced at her and said a shade apologetically, 'I almost did, then I realised it wasn't my place to say anything. I thought he'd prefer to tell you himself.' After a moment, and with another sideways glance, he ventured, 'Do you mind?'

'About what?' asked Lyall.

'About your husband's generosity?'

'Good gracious, no! I think it's wonderful of him.'

The ginger-haired man looked relieved.

To get off the subject which seemed to have worried him, she queried, 'How's Grandad? I thought he looked a bit down this morning.'

'He had a big day yesterday,' Duggan agreed. 'That's why I thought a complete twenty-four hours in bed with only light meals would be a good idea. But don't worry yourself. He's OK, really.'

When they reached the penthouse, Lyall had a hot bath to soak the tiredness out of her limbs, and let her mind drift. She was looking forward to the evening, to Jordan coming home, with all the eagerness of a young Juliet waiting for Romeo. She wanted to hear his voice, to see his face, and, she hoped, find the same kind of look in his eyes she'd glimpsed that morning when he'd lifted her palm to his lips.

When she had put on a dress of misty violet that Jordan had once remarked he liked, and taken special care with her hair and make-up, she went along to see Joe. Popping her head round his bedroom door, she found him lying back on his pillows, his mouth a little open, snoring peacefully. Lying on the coverlet by his side was a copy of Jerome K. Jerome's *Three Men in a Boat.* It had always been one of his favourite books (and hers too, for that matter) which he re-read from time to time. Smiling, she withdrew quietly and went back to the living-room.

Wilkes was moving about in the dining recess, soft-footed

as ever, setting the table for four.

'Are Mr Duggan and my grandfather dining with us after all?' asked Lyall.

'No, Madam,' Wilkes answered with the merest hint of reproof. 'I understand the master is bringing home guests.'

'Oh, yes, of course.' How stupid. He'd told her so that morning, but so much had happened afterwards it had gone right out of her head. Her rosy visions of herself and Jordan sitting together and talking, *really* talking, vanished. But there was always tomorrow, she consoled herself.

A moment or so later she heard the soft hum of the lift and, bracing herself, went into the foyer. The doors slid aside and three people stepped out: a blonde woman, strikingly dressed and elegant, talking to a short, thickset man with crisp brown hair and merry dark eyes, while Jordan brought up at the rear.

The woman's face was oddly familiar, but it wasn't until the thickset man addressed her as Nancy that Lyall realised why.

She was the blonde in the snapshot.

Despite the jolt that, like a shock of electricity, almost stopped her heart, somehow Lyall kept a smile fixed on her lips while Jordan put an arm around her slender waist and said, 'Allow me to introduce my wife . . . Lyall, this is Mrs Nancy Jepson, and her company boss, Bruce Mantell.'

The two women exchanged polite greetings, and Lyall thought bleakly that Nancy Jepson was one of the most beautiful creatures she'd ever seen. There was nothing artificial about her, either; it was the genuine beauty of naturally blonde hair and deep blue eyes, a dazzling smile and a glowing complexion.

Bruce Mantell stepped forward to take Lyall's hand and,

in an unexpectedly French manner, raise it to his lips. Mantell was an attractive man, with the slightly battered looks of a pugilist and all the charm of a Sacha Distel. He had a voice like rich velvet, which contrasted oddly with his Bronx accent, and his brown eyes were so dark they looked almost black. Lyall found herself warming to him straight away.

When Wilkes had deftly removed their outdoor things, Jordan led them through to the lounge. Over a pre-dinner drink, while the other three talked and Lyall mostly listened, she found, as she had already surmised, that these were the 'friends' Jordan had dined with the previous evening.

During the conversation it emerged that Nancy was a widow. Apparently, Robert Jepson, who had died some years before of a heart attack, had been very much older than her. But she spoke of him with respect and affection, and a genuine regret that he was no longer here.

As well as beauty, Nancy had character and charm, and Lyall was surprised to realise she would have liked the other woman enormously if the circumstances had been different and she hadn't felt so bitterly jealous.

It was plain, to Lyall at least, how Nancy felt about Jordan. Though she talked and smiled, beneath the bright mask there was such sadness and desolation that Lyall felt sorry for her. It must be heartbreaking to find the man you love, whose mistress you are, whose wife you are hoping to be, has suddenly married somone else.

Though, perhaps, by now, he'd told her how things were and asked her to carry on with the liaison. Lyall flinched away from that thought. But even if he had, it must hurt Nancy to have to share him. Would half a loaf seem better than no bread? Surely it must depend on how desperate she was not to lose him completely.

Over the meal two separate conversations developed. Nancy and Jordan talked about the business scene in London, while Bruce Mantell was riding what Lyall judged to be his favourite hobby-horse.

'I'm what you might call a fitness freak, I guess. There's a gym just along the block and I work out each day for at least an hour . . .'

He related some of the incidents which had taken place there with a quirky humour that, in spite of everything, kept her chuckling. She tried to avoid looking at the blonde and the peat-dark head so close together. But several times she was aware that Jordan stared across at them before, a frown drawing his brows together, he returned to his conversation.

Wilkes had provided an excellent meal, but Lyall was only too thankful to find it finally at an end. When coffee was served they moved in front of the fire to drink it, while Jordan led the talk into more general channels.

Lyall was refilling one of the dainty cups when Jordan broke off what he was saying to demand abruptly, 'Where's your ring?'

She followed his gaze to the fourth finger of her left hand, bare save for her wedding band. 'When I went to St Thomas's yesterday morning I gave it to Wilkes to put safely away.' Holding his gaze, she asked sweetly, 'Did you think I'd sold it?'

The other two laughed, but Jordan's mouth tightened ominously.

As soon as the coffee and liqueurs were drunk, Bruce Mantell said regretfully that they ought to be going.

'Tomorrow we have to make an early start. We've only got another couple of days in London before we're off to Paris and Rome.'

'Then where?' asked Jordan.

'Back home.' It was Nancy who answered, adding with an eagerness she couldn't altogether disguise, 'Have you any plans to come over to the States?'

'No immediate plans,' Jordan replied. 'But it's always on the cards.'

When they finally rose to go, he wouldn't hear of them getting a taxi, but insisted on driving them back to their hotel. As Lyall said her goodbyes she was aware that Nancy, though she had hidden it well, was as eager to go as she was to have her gone. Only Bruce seemed oblivious to any undercurrents.

After an exhausting day, the evening had been a strain, and Lyall, feeling shattered, went straight to bed. Though she tried to relax, sleep steadfastly refused to come, and she lay staring wide-eyed into the darkness.

She'd had such high hopes that things between Jordan and herself might be improving, but he'd dashed them to the ground by bringing home his mistress. Why had he done it? It seemed so unnecessarily cruel to them both.

When he got back, she decided, she'd try to talk to him. Though she'd annoyed him with her taunt about selling the ring, surely he'd talk to her? And if he did, perhaps they could recapture the rapport they had shared earlier . . .

For a while some shred of hope kept her spirits up, but as the hours dragged past on crippled feet she was forced to admit what maybe she had known from the start: he wasn't going to come.

Was he with Nancy? she wondered miserably, while the

talons of jealousy scored deep. If he was, there was absolutely nothing she could do about it. She had no hold on him, no real place in his life.

A ghostly dawn was lightening the eastern sky and a sparrow practising his first sleepy chirps before Lyall finally fell asleep.

When she awoke it was gone nine, and it was clear that she had slept alone. As soon as she had washed and dressed she went in search of Wilkes and, keeping her voice casual, asked if he knew where Jordan was.

'The master left immediately after breakfast,' the manservant informed her. 'He was unable to indicate precisely when he'd be home, though he did say not to expect him early.'

'Oh, thank you, Wilkes.' Lyall smiled, but her heart was like a stone.

'You look a bit peaky, lass,' remarked Joe when she went along to say good morning and tell Duggan she was ready. 'Maybe you're overdoing it.'

'Of course I'm not,' she denied brightly. 'Anyway, this is my last day as cook. Just before I left yesterday, Amy told me Mrs Simpson should be back tomorrow.'

'That's just as well.' Duggan put his oar in. 'You look so rough I'll soon have Mr Jameson after me. Are you certain you feel up to going in today? Because if you're not sure . . .'

'Quite sure,' Lyall told him. Any amount of work would be preferable to remaining unoccupied.

That afternoon, as she was leaving, Amy thanked her sincerely and said, 'You've worked like a Trojan, so you have. Now take a rest for a few days. You look as if you could do with it. But any time you've an hour or two to spare, we're only too grateful for some help.'

'I'll remember that,' promised Lyall, and meant it.

When they got back to the penthouse the white Porsche had been delivered, which satisfied Wilkes but failed to raise Lyall's spirits a jot. Trapped in a kind of vacuum, her thoughts tumbling over and over like clothes in a drier, she just waited for Jordan to come home.

That evening, when dinner was ready and there was still no sign of him, Wilkes, without being asked, set the table in Joe's room for three. So her grandfather wouldn't wonder, Lyall said vaguely that Jordan had an evening meeting, and was pleased when Joe didn't pursue the matter.

As soon as the meal was over, seeing he was tired, Lyall kissed him, said her goodnights, and went back to the main living-room.

She took a book from the shelves and made an effort to read, but her eyes would hardly stay open. When Jordan still hadn't come home and the clock struck ten, she gave in and took herself off to bed. She slept almost immediately, although it was a troubled sleep which gave her very little real rest.

Next morning she opened heavy eyes to find she had once more slept alone, but the door to the dressing-room was ajar. Pushing it wider, she looked inside. Jordan had slept in there. She felt a real sense of despair. It seemed he no longer even wanted her while Nancy was available.

She was still standing in the doorway when Jordan came out of the bathroom, freshly showered and shaved and wearing a short white towelling robe. 'Were you planning to go to the centre today?' he asked, with a cool politeness that she found chilling.

She'd been longing to talk to him, but now he was there

her throat was so tight that no words would come. She just stared at him.

Fastening the belt of the robe around his lean waist, he repeated the question.

'No . . .' She swallowed. 'Mrs Simpson should be back. I . . . I'd like to go and see Mitch.' When he didn't say anything, she stumbled on, 'The flat's expensive and before too long she'll have to find someone to share it, so I ought to go and move the rest of my things.'

He nodded briefly and disappeared into the dressing-room, closing the door.

Determined not to cry, Lyall washed and dressed, and tried to erect a screen of composure to hide behind. Finally she managed it.

When she got to the breakfast table Jordan was already there, informally dressed in fawn trousers and a brown shirt. His hair, parted on the left and brushed back, had by this time started to dry into loose curls. He looked very handsome and she longed for him to smile at her.

He didn't. He merely rose courteously and pulled out a chair. There was a selection of food keeping hot on the sideboard, but she refused a cooked breakfast and helped herself to toast and marmalade before pouring coffee for them both.

'Do you want to go to Buckton Place this morning?' asked Jordan, as he served himself with grilled bacon and fried eggs. 'If so, I'll drive you over. You'll need some help if you've things to move.' He spoke with distant civility.

She thanked him as she would have done a stranger.

The day was cold, bright, and blustery, a gay, gypsy kind of day. As they drove across town sunshine gilded the buildings and lay along the streets like yellow ribbons, while a vagabond wind fluttered window blinds and awnings.

Mitch answered the door to Jordan's ring and cried, 'Well, look who's here! So what are you two doing back already? No, don't tell me, I can guess. But Joe's fine, isn't he? I went over last Sunday for an hour, and I thought he looked a new man . . .' Still talking, she led the way inside.

The sight of the old flat, shabby and homely, brought a lump to Lyall's throat. She swallowed past it and turned to find Jordan watching her closely. He seemed to know exactly what she was feeling, and she looked sharply away, resenting the easy way he could walk in and out of her privacy, while allowing her no access to his thoughts.

'I expect you've come for your belongings,' Mitch was saying. 'I've put most of your books and oddments into cardboard boxes. But there's still some clothes and things in your bedroom.'

When everything had been packed and Jordan had carried the boxes down to the car, Mitch made a pot of coffee and they sat around the electric fire drinking it.

Jordan seemed to have relaxed, and he joined in the conversation easily enough. 'What's it like, being on your own?' he asked Mitch, stretching his long legs towards the fire.

'To tell you the truth, I can't seem to settle,' the blonde girl admitted. 'I've missed Lyall a lot.'

'Have you found anyone to share with yet?'

She shook her bright gold curls. 'I haven't even tried. I know from past experience that it isn't easy to find a flatmate you can be sure of getting along with. And I'm rather hoping I won't need one, if everything goes according to plan.' She gave them one of her 'a nod's as good as a wink to a blind horse' looks.

'Don't say your Great-Aunt Jenny's finally died and left you that fortune?' Lyall asked lightly. 'Great-Aunt Jenny's fortune' had been a long-standing joke between the two girls.

Mitch laughed. 'No, the old dear's still going strong, hale and hearty at ninety-three. She'll probably reach a hundred at least before she pops her clogs.'

Jordan laughed with a flash of excellent white teeth, and suggested, 'Then you've had a win on the pools and you're considering buying a house in Park Lane?'

'Should be even better than that when it happens,' said Mitch mysteriously. She refilled the coffee-cups and changed the subject to ask, 'Do you think Jameson's might be in the market for an electronics wizard?'

Jordan raised a dark brow. 'Why, do you know one?'

'David's got about as far as he can with Galton's and he'd like to move into the fibre optics field.'

'We're doing a great deal of research into fibre optic communications. If he's interested, ask him to come and see me as soon as possible,' said Jordan.

Mitch pursed her lips thoughtfully. 'He's taking me to Le Bistro tonight for a meal . . . I don't suppose you two would care to come along and make it a foursome?'

Lyall had braced herself for a cool refusal when Jordan replied, 'If David's agreeable, be my guests and we'll go to Kershaw's.'

Kershaw's was a small, exclusive restaurant just off Hyde Park with an élite clientéle. No one who wasn't personally known to the propietor stood a chance of getting a table, no matter what his rank or financial status.

Mitch gave an expressive whistle and said with

certainty, 'He'll be *delighted*.' Then her brow furrowed. 'But I don't know if I've got anything posh enough for a place like Kershaw's . . . Unless I wear the dress I bought for my engagement.'

'Engagement?' exclaimed Lyall. 'When did you get engaged?'

'Well, he hasn't actually asked me yet,' Mitch admitted. 'But he's teetering on the brink. All he needs is a tiny push, which I'm all set to give him. That's why I'm not looking for a new flatmate. I've had my fill of being a bachelor girl, and a short engagement with just enough time to buy a trousseau and plan the wedding will suit me fine. Yes . . .' she murmured thoughtfully, '*that* might be the answer. Sort of killing two birds with one stone—though I've nothing against birds. If I wear the dress to go to Kershaw's . . .'

Jordan grinned and agreed, 'After a good meal, and a glass or two of champagne to soften him up . . .'

'I'll invite you all back for coffee . . .'

'But *we'll* be sure not to come.'

'That's the idea,' Mitch approved. And, laughing, the two conspirators saluted each other with their coffee-cups. 'Look,' she went on after a pause, 'I know Kershaw's is pretty snooty, and I don't want to let you down. If I put the dress on you can give me an honest opinion as to whether it's suitable. If it isn't, I shall just have to go shopping for something else. It's no use borrowing a horse, my hair's too short to go as Lady Godiva . . .'

She dashed off, to return quite quickly wearing a daring creation in poppy-red. It clung to her well rounded curves like a second skin, yet the overall effect was sophisticated and daringly elegant, rather than cheap.

'Very eye-catching,' commented Jordan.

Mitch looked at him suspiciously. 'If you mean it won't do . . .'

'I don't mean anything of the kind,' he denied firmly. 'You have the face and figure to carry it off to perfection. If *that* doesn't clinch it with the boyfriend, he has no red blood in his veins.'

Mitch visibly melted. Then, heading for the bedroom again, she said over her shoulder to Lyall, 'I thought I'd wear this with it, if you don't mind. It's the one you lent me ages ago. I'd put it in my top drawer and somehow it got pushed to the back . . .' Still talking, she returned sporting a two-inch-wide diamond bracelet on her right wrist. 'It isn't the kind of thing you can wear every day, and I'd forgotten about it until . . .'

Lyall drew a deep, painful breath, and Mitch stopped in mid-sentence.

Jordan turned to Lyall and in a voice devoid of emotion said, 'I take it that's something Paul gave you?'

Her anguished expression was answer enough.

Disconcerted, Mitch began, 'I'm terribly sorry, have I . . .'

'It's all right, really.' Lyall managed to find her voice. 'Jordan knows all about Paul's gifts.'

'Thank the Lord for that!' exclaimed Mitch with pious fervour. 'For a moment I thought I'd made the *faux pas* of the century!'

'May I see the bracelet?' asked Jordan.

After a glance at Lyall, Mitch unclasped the sparkling thing and handed it to him.

'It looks a pretty expensive item to leave lying around in a drawer,' he remarked.

'It looks good, but they're not real stones,' Mitch told him cheerfully.

Sharply he demanded. 'What makes you so sure?'

'Because Paul said they weren't.'

Jordan gave her a swift, authoratitive glance. 'Tell me about it.'

Loyal to her fingertips, the blonde girl looked at Lyall, unwilling to go any further without her say-so.

'Go on,' Lyall said steadily. 'I'd like you to tell him the whole truth.'

Mitch's forget-me-not blue eyes turned to Jordan's dark, powerful face. 'All right, just give me a minute to get the glad-rags off.'

'Thank you,' Jordan said quietly, and handed her back the bracelet.

She reappeared in a very short time, dressed once more in faded jeans and a blue fluffy jumper, the sleeves pushed up to her elbows. Sitting down opposite Jordan, she began without further delay.

'I don't know whether Lyall's told you, but Paul's gifts always made her uncomfortable. She didn't want him to keep spending his money on her, but she couldn't seem to stop him. Every time she said "no more", and every time he promised it would be the last. But he never kept his word. I don't believe he ever meant to.

'He was like a child, so eager to please her that she couldn't bear to hurt his feelings. But when he tried to give her the bracelet, she stuck her toes in and told him plainly that she wouldn't take it . . .' Mitch broke off. 'You know,' she said ruefully, 'this sounds as if I was always eavesdropping, but I wasn't, honestly.' This last was addressed to Lyall. Turning back to Jordan, she went on,

'The walls in this place are paper-thin and it's difficult *not* to overhear.

'Anyway, I was in my bedroom getting ready for a date when I heard him say, 'Don't be silly, sweetie, it looks OK, but they're not diamonds. I only wish I could afford to buy you the real thing.'

There was a long silence before Jordan said slowly, 'I'd like you to tell me about Paul . . . What did you think of him?'

Mitch gave him a wary look. 'Why do you want to know?'

'I'm curious,' he admitted. 'Lyall's told me quite a bit, but I'd like an unbiased opinion. I believe you're honest, and you're shrewd enough to make a good judge of character.'

Had he planned this? Lyall wondered. Was this why he had offered to bring her?

With a little shrug, Mitch began. 'He was a good-looking boy, charming in a lot of ways, but very young for his age and basically weak. He was obsessed with Lyall from the word go. It was like a sickness, it wasn't *normal* . . .'

His tawny eyes on her face, Jordan listened without speaking or moving.

'. . . He wanted her to love him, if you can call such an obsession love, and I think he did everything he could to buy her love. When she finally realised how things were and tried to let him down gently, he clung like a limpet.

'By that time she'd got genuinely fond of him and she couldn't bear the thought of hurting him. That was her weakness, and he was clever enough to realise that and exploit it to the full.

'If she'd listened to me she would have told him "on your bike!" when he started to come on too strong. Frankly, he was unstable, and he made her life a misery. His moods were frightening; he was either high as a kite or in the depths of despair. Thinking about it since, I've often wondered if he was on drugs . . .'

Jordan's head jerked a little, but he made no comment.

'That's all really,' Mitch went on after a moment. 'It was tragic the way he died, and I was very sorry. But I was more sorry for Lyall. She even started blaming herself, feeling guilty that she hadn't been able to love him the way he'd wanted her to. That's why I was so damned glad when she met you. You were so utterly different, and Paul had given her so much hassle . . .'

Jordan got to his feet and, a dark flush lying along his high cheekbones, went to stand by the window. Looking out across the square, he was silent for so long that Lyall found the tension almost unbearable.

At last he turned and asked harshly, 'You know she sold his gifts?' There was censure in his tone.

'Yes, I know,' Mitch answered. 'And I don't blame her a bit. She'd been under a great deal of pressure, and she *had* to have that ground-floor flat for when her grandfather came out of hospital. Otherwise, I know she wouldn't have parted with them, even though they *were* forced on her.'

There was another lengthy silence after Mitch had stopped speaking, then Jordan said formally, 'Thank you. That was very enlightening. Now I feel I owe you an explanation. I would have had no right to ask about something which happened before Lyall met me, except for one thing: Paul was my foster-brother.'

Mitch's mouth fell open and her blue eyes rounded. She looked at Lyall, who, for the most part, had been sitting staring down at her clenched hands, and said almost accusingly, 'You never told me a word about it.'

'Lyall didn't know until after the wedding,' Jordan explained quietly. 'When I brought Paul into the firm we kept our relationship under wraps, because I suspected industrial espionage and he was to be my watchdog while I was away.

'When I went to the States, he hadn't met Lyall, but he wrote to me about her. Her told me he was mad about her, and had asked her to marry him. He said she was the most hauntingly beautiful woman he'd ever seen.'

'So that's why you were so keen to meet her?' exclaimed Mitch.

'That's why.'

Frowning, the blonde girl asked, 'But why didn't you tell her you were Paul's foster-brother?'

'I decided to get to know her first. I wanted to find out what kind of woman had bewitched him so completely.'

'And by the time you knew . . .'

Jordan nodded. 'She'd bewitched me too.'

A romantic at heart, Mitch sighed. 'But about Paul . . . I'm sorry if I . . .'

'Don't be sorry,' said Jordan. 'I wanted a truthful answer. I always knew Paul was weak, but sometimes it takes a complete outsider to put things in perspective. Now, about tonight, what arrangements have you made?'

'Well, David's coming here at seven.'

'So if I pick you up about seven-thirty, say dinner eight-thirty?'

'Marvellous!' Mitch's baby-blue eyes sparkled.

When the two girls had hugged each other, Jordan helped Lyall into her coat and escorted her down the stairs, a hand beneath her elbow. He settled her in the car like some polite but distant stranger, and drove back to Montana House without speaking, his mouth a thin line, his dark face sombre.

Had he believed Mitch? Lyall wondered. She rather thought he had. But would it make any real difference to his feelings for *her*? Would it be possible to slough off the habit of hate? And if he stopped hating her, what then? His reason for marrying her had been revenge. If he was satisfied that reason was no longer valid, where would that leave them?

CHAPTER TEN

WHEN they reached the penthouse, Jordan asked Wilkes to bring the cartons from the car, adding, 'The ones full of books are quite heavy. If you need any help, don't hesitate to ask Duggan.'

Then, to Lyall he said with cool civility, 'If you'll excuse me, I won't be joining you for lunch—I have things to do. Can you be ready by about seven tonight?'

Without waiting for an answer he strode away, leaving her staring after him, stricken. She had hoped they would talk so she could find out what he was thinking, feeling. His abrupt departure left her abandoned in a kind of emotional limbo.

Perhaps Wilkes guessed something of what she was feeling, because he displayed a genuine, though unobtrusive, kindness, proposing a shade diffidently that she join her grandfather for lunch.

'Then afterwards,' he gave a little cough, 'I will be happy to help with the arranging of Madam's books.'

Lyall accepted the suggestion gratefully and, not careless of any kindness shown to her, thanked him with one of her lovely, luminous smiles, which, without her knowing it, made him her slave for life.

After lunch, while Joe had his rest, she unpacked the cartons, and with Wilkes's help began to arrange the books on the shelves in one of the alcoves at the far end of the living-room. While they worked he confessed to being 'partial to books', and from a chance remark she discovered that he was a Dorothy Sayers fan. Her mental picture of who he'd modelled himself on changed from Jeeves to Bunter.

'If there's any book you'd like to borrow, just help yourself,' she told him.

He thanked her gravely and, when everything was tidy and the cartons had been disposed of, disappeared kitchenwards with a copy of *Busman's Honeymoon* tucked beneath his arm.

Unwilling to be alone with her thoughts, Lyall went along to join her grandfather and Duggan. 'Jordan still has some work to catch up on,' she said with a determinedly cheerful air.

'I know, lass,' said Joe. 'He came along for a word before he went out.'

So it was only *her* he was avoiding so assiduously.

Hiding her unhappiness beneath a bright mask, she spent the afternoon with them, playing a three-handed card game. Luck was so doggedly on her side that she easily won both their piles of sticky black Pontefract cakes which they were using as stake money. When they grumbled she said with mock severity, 'You shouldn't gamble if you're not prepared to lose. In any case, you've eaten half of them.'

Just before seven o'clock, Lyall was waiting in the living-room, showered and changed all ready for the evening. Having a very limited choice, she had put on the green and grey chiffon dress and grey strappy sandals she had been wearing the first time she had met Jordan.

An odd nervousness had made her usually quite competent fingers all thumbs, and after several abortive attempts to put up her hair she had left it loose. Careful make-up had done a lot to help disguise her paleness, and given her oval face a soft glow. She looked self-possessed and very lovely. Only her shadowed green eyes betrayed her insecurity and inner tension.

There had been no sign of Jordan but, presumably on his instructions, Wilkes had produced her engagement ring before pouring her a fruit juice cocktail. His thinning hair neatly combed to hide his balding head, his grey-blue eyes kindly, he had informed her, 'The master is home, but I'm given to understand he's awaiting an important phone call. He should be joining you shortly.'

It was practically seven-fifteen before Jordan appeared in the doorway, looking devastatingly handsome in impeccable evening clothes. However could she have once considered him too rugged to be handsome?

'Have you had your phone call?' she asked for something to say.

'I'm afraid not,' he answered shortly.

She had wondered if he might want her to wear the emerald necklace, but with scarcely a glance he helped her into her short jacket and led her to the lift.

The wind had followed the sun over the edge of the world, and the night was calm and starry. Lyall found herself remembering that first evening they'd met, and how Jordan had told her about the angels who tend the star-lamps. A half-smile on her lips, she turned towards him, but keeping his eyes on the road he ignored her except to ask, 'Warm enough?'

'Yes, thank you.' Rebuffed, she gazed blindly through the windscreen. Instead of stars, she watched the lights of the oncoming traffic and the red tail-lamps of the vehicle in front and, her heart like lead, wondered how she was ever going to get through the evening.

When they reached Buckton Place, they drew up behind David's elderly black Mini GT and climbed the uncarpeted stairs to the second-floor flat.

Mitch opened the door to Jordan's ring with an alacrity which suggested she had been hovering behind it. She was wearing the poppy-red dress, but a gold bangle in place of the 'diamond' bracelet. Smiling, she ushered them inside and introduced David to Jordan; then, while they shook hands, she produced a quite passable sherry.

As they drank, the two men chatted, measuring each other up. David, openly, as was his style, Jordan, more subtly. He had emerged now from his cocoon of silence, and appeared all set to play the perfect host and ensure the success of the evening.

Lyall watched them as they stood together. David, fair and smiling, boyish and quite uncomplicated, his chocolate-brown eyes eager, looked thinner and more gangling than ever beside Jordan's mature width of chest and shoulder. Jordan, dark and unsmiling, his tawny, long-lashed eyes brilliant, looked what he was, a tough, complex man, a man to be reckoned with. Yet David, Lyall saw, was quick and intelligent and, without being either pushy or over-confident, not only held his own, but several times won a round. Silently she cheered him on.

Jordan drove them to Kershaw's, while David kept them entertained with a droll account of a weekend spent at his parents' home. 'Mother, bless her heart, trying to be thoroughly modern and unshockable, said if we wanted to share a room she'd quite understand. After Mitch had disabused her, she was so delighted to have her good old-fashioned standards back that I was lucky not to have been banished to the garage . . .'

Kershaw's was everything that Lyall had expected, and more. The lilac and white décor was quietly elegant, the pearl-grey carpet soft as smoke beneath their feet, the clientéle well dressed and clearly from the upper echelon. After an aperitif at the bar, they were shown to a candlelit table. Though the room was very large, there were only half a dozen tables in all, set well apart and screened from their immediate neighbours by banks of flowers and foliage. The atmosphere was relaxed, the service superb, the food and vintage wines incomparable.

It soon became apparent that the two men, dissimilar as they were, had hit it off. They talked easily over a wide range of subjects before getting to electronics, where, despite Jordan's wide knowledge of up-to-date methods and technology, David was able to give a good account of himself.

'He's clever,' Lyall remarked in an undertone to Mitch.

'He's a fool,' said Mitch fondly. 'You know we went to Hampshire last Saturday to visit his parents? Well, on the way back we saw this little old lady by the side of the road. She was standing against an old Morris Minor wringing her hands. We stopped and David called out, "Something wrong?".

'She pointed to the nearside front wheel and wailed, "Whatever shall I do? I've got a flat tyre."'

'He went over to look, then do you know what the idiot said? "Don't worry about it, love, it's only flat at the bottom."'

'He changed the wheel for her, of course, but all the time he was doing it she gave him a wide berth, and from the way she looked at him I'm sure she was convinced he was an escaped lunatic.'

Lyall laughed, a husky, attractive sound that brought Jordan's head round. Those gold-flecked eyes, which still gave her a jolt when she looked into them, met and held hers for a moment. Then, without the slightest smile lighting their depths, he looked away. She felt an acute sense of loss, of rejection, and briefly her composure slipped, revealing the misery beneath the calm mask.

When the sweet plates had been removed and they were waiting for coffee to be served, Mitch picked up her gold-beaded bag and asked, 'Coming to freshen up?'

Together the women walked to the luxurious ivory and pink powder-room. All the small gilt chairs in front of the discreetly lit mirrors were empty, and as they sat down side by side Mitch asked bluntly, 'What's wrong?'

Lyall smiled brightly and said, 'Nothing's wrong.'

Far from satisfied, Mitch shook her curly head. 'Pull the other one, it's got bells on it. Come on now, something's wrong. You look anything but happy.' Then, like a rapier thrust, 'Has Jordan been giving you a rough time?'

The thrust found its mark. Suddenly, to Lyall's horror, tears came. She closed her eyes tightly in an effort to hold them back, but they squeezed themselves beneath her lids and rolled down her ckeeks.

'Oh, *love*!' Mitch exclaimed.

Lyall fought for control and after a minute dredged up a shaky smile. 'It's all right. The last thing I want to do is spoil the evening. I'm just . . . just a bit overwrought.'

'Was Jordan angry over what I said about Paul?' Mitch demanded. 'Did he take it out on you?'

'No . . . no.'

'If I thought it was my fault . . .'

'No, it isn't your fault, truly. What you told him was the truth, and he did ask.' Then, with an overwhelming urge to confide in her friend, Lyall blurted out, 'The fact is, Jordan never loved me. Because of all those presents, he believed I was just a heartless gold-digger who'd only used Paul. He blamed me for his death. I know it sounds silly and melodramatic, but he only married me because he wanted to make me as miserable as he thought I'd made Paul.'

'Oh, my God!' Mitch sounded staggered. 'But didn't you tell him how it was?'

'Of course I did. He wouldn't believe me.'

Mitch worried her lips. 'Surely after this morning he must realise he was mistaken?'

'I don't know,' Lyall admitted bleakly. 'It depends how much he accepted as the truth.'

'Didn't he say anything once you were alone?'

Lyall shook her head. 'He's hardly spoken to me since we left the flat.'

'I can't understand it,' muttered Mitch. 'I could have sworn he was mad about you.'

'He *hates* me,' Lyall whispered brokenly.

'I don't believe it,' Mitch argued stoutly. 'He may have *wanted* to hate you, but I've seen the way he looks at you.' Then, shrewdly, 'How do you feel about him now?'

'At first I felt very bitter and I tried to tell myself I hated him . . .'

'But you don't?'

'No.' The word was barely audible. 'Oh, Mitch, what am I going to do?' It was a cry of despair.

'Hang on,' advised Mitch. 'Give him time to come to terms with the mess he's made of things, and see how he really feels. You're his wife. It's my bet he'll want to keep it that way.'

'But there's someone else . . . another woman . . .'

'Is he still seeing her?'

'I think so.'

'Well, my advice is don't give up too easily. If you love him, fight for him. If this other woman had meant anything to him, surely he'd have married *her*.'

As Mitch finished speaking, the pink-satin-lined door opened and two stout ladies, looking like dowager duchesses, sailed in on a wave of French perfume.

'And do you think Georgie would behave?' the elder one was crying dramatically. 'He actually nipped poor Roderick . . .'

While Mitch made a pretence of patting her halo of blonde curls into place, Lyall hastily dried her eyes and repaired her make-up.

As they left the marshmallow atmosphere, Mitch gave her arm a comforting squeeze, and they walked back to their table debating what, or who, Georgie and Roderick were. Lyall plumped for poodle and husband, while Mitch cynically suggested that as the dowager had said, '*poor* Roderick' they were more likely to be both poodles.

When they reached the table the two men rose and David complained good-naturedly, 'We were just thinking of sending a search-party. It beats me what women find to *do* for that length of time. Men never dawdle about like that.'

'I don't honestly know why men think they're so perfect,' Mitch said tartly.

David and Jordan exchanged glances of amusement. 'Perhaps because we *are*,' David murmured smugly, as the women were seated.

Mitch delivered herself of an 'oh, give me strength' look and attacked from an unexpected angle. 'Your mother says you snore.' Then, in alarm, 'Do you?'

David grinned. 'Only when I'm asleep.'

Over coffee and liqueurs the talk became general, and if Lyall played with the stem of her glass, saying little, and Mitch was unusually thoughtful, neither of the men seemed to notice.

The remainder of the evening passed pleasantly enough, and both Mitch and David agreed that Kershaw's more than lived up to its reputation. They left just before midnight and drove leisurely to Buckton Place. When they drew up outside the flat, Mitch invited them in for more coffee.

True to his word, Jordan declined politely, before advising David, 'Go and see Jim Taylor the first chance you get. He's in charge of the department you're interested in. You can tell him I sent you, though he's a man who won't be swayed by that. If he doesn't think he can use you he'll say so. But my guess is he will be able to.'

'Thanks,' David said gratefully. 'And thanks for a grand evening.' Then, a shade hesitantly, 'Perhaps we can do it again some time? I can't offer anything like Kershaw's, but next time I'll make the arrangements, and you must be our guests.'

'We'll look forward to it.' Jordan sounded as if he meant it. As Mitch got out he turned his head to murmur, 'Good luck.'

'I'll invite you to the wedding,' she promised, *sotto voce.*

Once they had dropped the other two, Jordan withdrew again, and Lyall, unable to find the courage to try to storm those mental barriers, sat in silence.

Though it was late when they reached the penthouse, Wilkes was waiting for them. As he took their coats he informed Jordan, 'A Mr Wood rang soon after you'd left. When I apprised him of the fact that you would be absent all evening, he called round to leave this package for your return.' His speech done, the manservant handed over a buff envelope.

Jordan took it with a word of thanks and, without even a glance in Lyall's direction, disappeared into the study.

She said goodnight to Wilkes, then, misery making her limbs like lead and her actions slow and clumsy, undressed and climbed into bed. Unable to sleep, she tossed restlessly, hoping Jordan would come, but knowing he wouldn't. Obviously he intended to spend the night in the dressing-room again. But why? What had turned him against her so completely after that momentary closeness?

When it was clear that sleep wasn't going to come, and no longer able to stand the pain of her thoughts, she got up and went in search of something to read. Pulling her white négligé around her, she padded barefoot across the carpet to the living-room. The door was closed but not latched. As she pushed it open she realised that the light was on.

Jordan was sitting by the dying embers of the fire in a pool of light shed by one of the standard lamps. He was leaning forward, his elbows on his knees, his head in his hands, his whole attitude one of despair.

It tore her apart to see a strong man like Jordan look so utterly beaten. Perhaps she made some slight sound, because he glanced up. She caught her breath, shocked by the bleakness in his eyes, the lines of pain around his well-cut mouth. He looked like a man who had been on the rack.

She wanted to run to him, to cradle his dark head against her breast, but, held back by the fear of rejection, she took a few steps forward and sank into the nearest chair.

'What is it?' she whispered. 'What's the matter?'

At first she thought he wasn't going to answer, then slowly, wearily he said, 'Since we've been back I've been doing some checking, talking to people who knew Paul. I hired a private detective to try and dig out the whole truth. I've just read his report. Your friend put her finger on it. Paul *was* on drugs—hard drugs, the damned young fool! That was where most of his money went. I know now it wasn't you who was bleeding him dry.'

Lyall made a soft little sound, almost like a sigh.

'I've been wrong about you all along the line.' Jordan's voice was rough with emotion. 'Even before we came back I was starting to wonder if I'd been mistaken. From our very first meeting, nothing I learnt fitted in with the image I had of you. Yet I couldn't, *wouldn't* believe you were as innocent as you looked.

'One of the things that shook me most was your gift of the paperweight. But even then I was too obsessed with your supposed guilt to fit the jigsaw together and look at the new picture forming—until that day at breakfast when we talked. But after all I'd done to you, I didn't want to believe I could have been wrong. Then when Mitch spoke the truth so bluntly, I *had* to believe it. I was shattered.'

There was silence, except for the ticking of the clock and a faint splash from the fountain. A half-burnt log settled with a rustle, sending a shower of bright sparks before crumbling into whitish ash.

Jordan lifted his head and looked at Lyall, at the silky dark hair, the jade-green eyes, the warm, generous mouth, the tension in her lovely face. Speaking with difficulty, he said, 'As soon as possible, I'll give you grounds for a divorce. I'll buy you a house or flat, whichever you prefer, and make sure you're financially secure so you won't need to work unless you want to. I suggest, if you're agreeable, that to give you some freedom you keep Duggan. I'll be responsible for his wages.'

His words had the same effect as a high-speed lift dropping her sharply downwards. She folded her arms across her stomach and pressed hard. So there it was, the end of all her hopes. He felt nothing for her, merely wanted to get rid of her as soon as he could with as little fuss as possible. To wipe the slate clean by providing for her and her grandfather.

When she didn't speak, Jordan added, 'Of course, you can stay on at the penthouse for as long as you need to.'

'What will you do?' She *had* to know.

'Go back to the States.'

Her heart jerked with the agony of the knife thrust. Bleeding to death inside, she needed the *coup de grâce*. 'Will . . . will you marry Nancy?'

'No,' he answered flatly.

Lyall stared down at her clenched hands and thought of Mitch's advice: 'Don't give up too easily. If you love him, fight for him.'

Huskily she asked, 'If you're not planning to marry again, why . . . why do you want to divorce me?' She swallowed past the hot glass clogging her throat. 'Do you still hate me?'

'Perhaps I hated the woman I thought you were, but I've never hated you. I tried to tell myself I did. But from the first moment I saw you, you enchanted me. You were so beautiful that at times I forgot my real reason for wanting to marry you.' His voice rough, he went on, 'The more I saw of you, the deeper I fell under your spell. I didn't want to love you, I felt as if I was betraying Paul, but I couldn't help it. You were so sweet and brave that I hated myself every time I hurt you, yet I seemed unable to stop.

'I can't give you back what I've taken from you, or wipe out all the pain and misery I've caused you. Dear God,' the words were almost a groan, 'I only wish I could!'

There was such anguish in his face that her eyes filled with tears.

'I know you loved me once. Joe told me what you'd said about following me to the ends of the earth. Love like that was more than I'd dared to hope or dream of finding. And I've thrown it all away . . .'

He brushed a hand over his eyes. 'I love you more than I ever thought it possible to love any woman. It's like tearing my heart out to let you go, but it's the only reparation I can make now I've made you hate me . . .'

Lyall's tears brimmed over and began to run down her cheeks. 'I don't hate you,' she denied strongly.

Jordan's head came up then, and he looked at her. 'I know I deserve it,' he said hoarsely, 'but don't play games with me. If there's the faintest chance of forgetting the past, of ever loving me again . . .'

She went down on her knees by his chair and put her arms around his neck. 'I know I said I hated you, but it wasn't true. I've never stopped loving you.'

In almost incredulous hope, he ordered, 'Say that again.'

'I've never stopped loving you,' she repeated with a sound half-way between a laugh and a sob.

With an incoherent murmur, his arms went around her

and gathered her close, his embrace so convulsive she could scarcely breathe. Then he was kissing her with a hunger that seemed to draw her very soul from her body.

His lips against her throat, he muttered, 'Oh, God, if you only knew how much I've wanted to do that! I've lain awake these past two nights, burning to hold you in my arms and kiss you.' Scooping her up, he lifted her on to his lap and began kissing her again.

'Why did you move into the dressing-room?' asked Lyall, when her mouth was momentarily freed.

'When I started to realise how wrong I'd been about you, it seemed the only thing to do. You'd said you hated me to touch you, and if I'd stayed in the same bed I wasn't sure I could trust myself to keep my hands off you.'

'I thought it was because of Nancy,' she confessed.

'Because of Nancy?' he echoed.

'I thought you'd been . . . seeing her.'

'As far as I was concerned, that was finished when I left the States.'

'Then why did you bring her here?' All the hurt she'd felt was there in her voice.

'I do believe you were jealous!' he crowed. As Lyall began indignantly to free herself from his arms he said hastily, 'All right, I'll tell you.' He stole a quick kiss. 'Bruce loves her and wants to marry her, but she wouldn't commit herself. I think she was still hoping . . .' He broke off, then went on levelly, 'The reason I invited her here was so she could *see* my wife, accept my marriage as a fact. She's a nice person, and I think Bruce is the right man for her. He'll make her happy when she eventually accepts him. But not half as happy as I'm determined to make you.'

He wiped away the dampness left by her tears, and kissed